A New Paige

Crawdad Beach Series (Book 8)

Lisa Buffaloe

A New Paige

Visit the author's website at https://lisabuffaloe.com.

Cover Design: JoAnn Durgin

ISBN: 978-1-957715-37-7 (eBook)
ISBN: 978-1-957715-38-4 (Paperback)
ISBN: 978-1-957715-39-1 (Hardcover)

A New Paige

*Sometimes, when you think you're running away,
you find you're running to God's perfect plan.*

For six years, Paige Clark dated the man she thought she'd marry. Instead, Devin had left her with regrets and a heartache her medical degree could never mend. When Paige was invited to join her favorite employer as he moved his practice to Crawdad Beach, she jumped at the opportunity to leave behind unwanted memories.

Quinn Young had not yet gotten over an unexpected life change when a great-aunt he barely knew passed away and left him her house and a cat to beat all cats, Sir Purrcevel. The last place Quinn thought he'd find himself was in the small town of Crawdad Beach. However, his choices were limited. Either move to his late aunt's house for six months and care for her cat or forfeit his inheritance.

Paige and Quinn aren't looking for companionship, but when a massive, mischievous cat causes their lives to intersect, a fun friendship forms. As romantic sparks fly, will their respective pasts keep them from new opportunities and second chances, or will they find a love that lasts forever?

Book 8 of the Crawdad Beach Series

Table of Contents

Chapter 1

Paige Clark turned up her music as loud as it would go and belted the words to the sad love song. Tears streamed down her cheeks as she drove the country back road.

This is *not* how she thought her life would go. Devin, the man she'd dated for six years, had made his choice, and that choice was not Paige. She hit the steering wheel. How could she have been so naive, stupid, ignorant, and clueless to have given Devin her heart and her everything in a relationship that went absolutely nowhere?

Paige choked back a sob. She was thirty-two, a successful nurse practitioner who should have her life together. Instead, she'd wasted years with a man who used her. And now her job was being relocated to some little town named after a crustacean. She could have stayed in Charlotte, but what was left for her now other than bad memories?

The doctor she'd worked with for years had decided to open a satellite medical office in Crawdad Beach, giving Paige a generous bonus to be part of his new adventure. Dr. Adam Abbott was more like a father and friend than her boss. He and his wife, Nancy, had become so close that Paige couldn't imagine working for anyone but him. Maybe a move was the best thing for her right now.

She'd leave the past behind, keep focused on her work, and forever forget about men.

Quinn Young couldn't understand why his great-aunt had left him her house in her will. The lawyer who contacted Quinn about the gift mentioned there was one caveat, which the lawyer said he'd explain once Quinn arrived. He'd taken his laptop so he could work while he was away from his apartment, flown to Charleston, and rented a car to drive to Crawdad Beach.

Besides a few interactions when he was a kid, he'd seen his aunt at his dad and grandad's funeral. Aunt Norma had hugged him tight and whispered in his ear that she was praying for him. Both times, Quinn sensed Norma meant her prayers weren't just for the grief of losing family members but for his life.

He couldn't imagine his aunt's estate would be worth much. His mom was as surprised as he was that Norma named him in her will. As far as they both knew, she'd lived in Crawdad Beach all her life and wasn't that wealthy. He pictured a tiny house filled with worthless, old things that he'd have to dispose of before he could put the house on the market. He just hoped she didn't have outstanding bills.

Summer sun warming his car, he drove along the brick-paved main street of Crawdad Beach lined with two-story brick buildings.

For a small town, it was surprisingly busy and had an interesting assortment of businesses. Besides a post office, the city had Knick Knacks Antique store, Curl and Dye Beauty Salon, Tiddlywinks Restaurant, Rolling in the Dough Bakery, loft apartments, Hotel de Crawdad, and a medical clinic that would be opening soon. Any town with a Crawdad as its mascot must have a sense of humor.

Quinn grinned at the sign in front of Doohickeys Hardware, which said they offered a wide range of hardware, building supplies, and whatever whatchamacallit needed. He chuckled.

He parked his rental car in front of the law office and ran his hand through his brown curly hair. It wasn't long, but he probably should have gotten a haircut. As he entered the building, he felt like he'd gone back in time with oak floors and wood paneling smelling of wood, leather, and old books.

"Good morning." A woman with short gray hair looked up from where she was working at her desk.

"Morning. I'm Quinn Young. I'm here about a will."

"Yes," The woman smiled. "Your aunt Norma was such a precious woman." She pointed to an open door behind her desk. "Go right in. Mr. McGee is expecting you."

Quinn thanked her and entered the office with bookshelves filled with law books. Two leather chairs faced a massive wood desk that looked to have been from the early 1900s.

A big man with white hair had his back to Quinn as he rummaged through a wood file cabinet. "Have a seat. I'll be right with you," the man said without looking up.

Quinn settled in a brown leather wingback chair and glanced around the office. Although crammed with books, the office was clean and even had a subtle lemony smell that reminded him of the furniture polish his mom used.

"There it is." The man placed the file on his desk and then held his hand toward Quinn. "I'm Carlton McGee. Welcome to Crawdad Beach. Your aunt told me so much about you."

He shook the man's outstretched hand. "She did?" How could that even be possible? They barely knew one another.

Carlton chuckled as he sat at his desk. "Oh yes, she spoke very highly of you."

Surely, the man didn't realize who he was. "You know. I'm Quinn Young."

"Oh, yes. You're Norma's great-nephew. You're thirty-two, have never been married, work from home, and currently live in Augusta, Georgia." The man's gaze settled on him.

Quinn fidgeted under the man's scrutiny. "That's correct." And way too strange. How did he know anything about him? Quinn hadn't married, but he'd dated many women and been engaged twice. Unfortunately, one woman wasn't faithful, and the other destroyed his reputation.

Carlton opened the file and then put on a pair of glasses as he looked over the paperwork. "I think you'll be pleased by what Norma is offering."

"Offering? I thought she just left me her house."

"That's correct. You're her sole heir. She left you her

house, car, accounts, and cat, Sir Purrcevel."

Quinn coughed a laugh. "Sir Purrcevel?"

"He's quite an animal. Very intelligent and weighs over twenty to thirty pounds. Norma's friends have been taking care of him. The sad thing is, Sir Purrcy hasn't purred since Norma passed." Carlton gave a mournful shake of his head. One of his eyebrows raised as he gazed at Quinn. "You do like cats, don't you?"

A twenty or thirty-pound cat? Surely, Carlton was being overdramatic. "I've never personally owned one, but my mom has two nice, decent cats."

"Well, good. That is one of Norma's requirements in her will that you tenderly love and care for Sir Purrcevel."

"Okay. I guess." Maybe he could give the cat to his mom.

"Now, let me tell you the rest," Carlton continued. "To receive the full inheritance, you must agree not only to lovingly care for her cat but also live in her home for six months and attend church every Sunday."

Carlton moved the documents toward him. "If you agree with the terms, you will be given twenty percent of Norma's financial accounts today, a stipend at the first of each month, and the rest at the end of six months, along with the deed of the house and all of her personal property."

Quinn rubbed the back of his neck. Why would he even consider moving to this little town? Her estate probably wasn't worth much anyway.

"By your hesitation," Carlton said. "I perceive you are not sure if you want to proceed. However, before you make a hasty decision, let me show you what Norma's accounts are worth today. Your aunt was a very wise investor." He handed Quinn a list of accounts from the bank and investment companies she had used.

Quinn looked at the amount and gulped as his eyebrows shot to his hairline. Living in Crawdad Beach was looking better by the minute.

Chapter 2

"**I** can't believe how nice this is." Paige walked next to Dr. Abbott and his wife, Nancy, as they showed her the new medical office. A reception area, exam rooms, and an x-ray machine were on the main level. The converted Main Street building still contained the original charm, yet with modern features and equipment.

"Everything should be ready in a few days," Nancy said. "We hired local builder Katherine Mitchell to complete the renovations for us. Katherine's an accomplished builder who turned several of the other downtown buildings into loft apartments, a bakery, and a hotel. Have you checked out your apartment?"

"Not yet. I looked at online photos but wanted to see how the office looked first. I'll stay at the Hotel de Crawdad tonight." Paige grinned at the funny name of the little boutique hotel.

"Remember, we're paying for your move and any expenses you might have."

"It's not a problem. You don't need to do that." The couple had always been generous with her, even paying beyond what most medical practices would pay for her position.

"We are bribing you." Dr. Abbott nudged Paige with his shoulder as they walked down the hall. "I can't imagine having my practice with anyone else."

"Paige, we appreciate you coming with us," Nancy said. "I fell in love with the little town last year, and now that our kids are grown, we were ready for a slower lifestyle. I know Crawdad Beach doesn't have as much to offer for a single person, but we hope you'll like living here."

"I'm not looking for nightlife," Paige said. After the fiasco with Devin, she wasn't looking for anything or anyone but some peace of mind. "I'm ready to stay busy with work, go home at night, and curl up with a good book."

"Did you see the library in the old railroad station, with the cute mural painted on the side?"

Paige grinned at Nancy's enthusiasm. "Yes, someone is a talented artist. I wonder who thought of a cartoon crawdad sitting on the beach reading a book?"

"I don't know, but it's so cute. Just wait until you visit the bakery and Tiddlywinks restaurant. They also use the little crawdad in their businesses."

"Maybe we should embrace the crustacean like the rest of the town," Dr. Abbott said. "For the reception area, we could hire the artist to paint a cartoon crawdad wearing a doctor's coat."

"That's such a great idea, honey." Nancy's blue eyes twinkled with her smile as she kissed her husband's cheek. "He could even have a little stethoscope around his neck."

"Excellent," he agreed. "Let's check with Katherine and

find out who could paint it for us."

A pang of jealousy made Paige turn away from the happily married couple. The Abbots had been together for over twenty-five years and still enjoyed one another's company.

Why couldn't she have a relationship like that? God had abandoned her, just like when her father drove off when Paige was twelve. Her dad died three years later in a drunk-driving car accident. What made it even worse was the fact that her dad was the drunk.

Paige sighed. As much as she preferred blaming God for her dad's failures and her feelings of abandonment, she knew that wasn't true. Her dad made his own bad choices, and she was the one who left God and ran into the arms of a man who left her with nothing but heartache and regrets. Why could she treat illness and injuries but was clueless on how to fix her broken, mixed-up heart?

"I can't wait to show you the upstairs," Nancy said as she practically bounced up the stairway.

Paige followed the couple to where the offices, storage, and a small break area were located.

Her life was in for significant changes, which was fine with her. She'd move soon into her new place, and once the office opened, she could settle into a predictable routine without worrying about men and relationship issues.

House key in hand, Quinn stood on the porch of the well-kept craftsman-style home that once belonged to his aunt. The lawn was well maintained, making it look as though someone still lived there.

Quinn tried to peek in the windows, but the curtains were drawn. The lawyer had warned him not to enter the house until Norma's friend, Chester, came over. Evidently, Sir Purrcevel could be irritable with newcomers.

"Hello!" A silver-haired gentleman walked toward him and stepped on the porch. "You must be Quinn. I'm Chester Taylor."

Quinn shook the man's hand. Chester's grip was surprisingly firmer than expected. "Yes, sir. Nice to meet you."

"Well, let's get you inside and introduce you to the master in charge of the premises." Chester held up a can of cat food. "I brought his favorite. You might want to make a note of what Sir Purrcevel likes. He is picky. Fortunately, our local store, Mitchell's Grocery, carries his brand."

"Sounds like the cat is spoiled."

"You have no idea." Chester chuckled as he unlocked the door. "Better let me go first." He flipped on the room lights and moved like a military guy as he walked around, his gaze sweeping back and forth. "The coast is clear. You might want to open the curtains. You don't want to get blindsided by an attack."

"Attack?" Quinn straightened as he checked around the room for any furry wild cats.

"Purrcevel has been known to do things like that before. The poor pizza guy swore he'd never deliver to this address again." He chuckled. "Thankfully, the new delivery man is a cat lover, so you're safe if you want to place an order."

"Good to know." Quinn pulled the drawstring on the curtains, and sunshine flooded the room, making the hardwood floors gleam in the sunlight. His aunt had surprisingly good taste. Quinn stood still as a feeling of calm and peace surrounded him. The family room contained a bluish/gray sofa, two wingback chairs in the same color, and a nice wooden coffee table. The house didn't smell musty or have a cat odor; instead, it had a faint scent of cinnamon.

"Sir Purrcevel. It's Chester." He motioned toward Quinn. "You might want to introduce yourself."

Quinn started to laugh until he saw Chester's serious expression. Might as well go along with the man. Quinn tried not to show how ridiculous he felt. "Sir Purrcevel. My name is Quinn Young. I'm Norma's great-nephew."

Chester leaned closer and whispered. "Mention you'll be staying here and caring for him."

"Right." Quinn turned back to the empty room. "Sir Purrcevel, I'll be moving in here and ensuring you get the food and love you need."

Chester gave him a thumbs up.

"So, what do we do now?"

"We wait." Chester stood like a military guy in the at-ease position.

Quinn tried not to roll his eyes at the ridiculousness of

standing and waiting for a cat.

Chester cleared his throat and motioned with his eyes toward the hallway.

The biggest, most massive cat Quinn had ever seen was moving toward them. He had long gray fur like a Persian, but his face and ears resembled a bobcat.

Sir Purrcevel jumped up on the back of one of the wingback chairs, his amber eyes squinting in displeasure as he stared at Quinn. The cat released a low, menacing, tear-your-face-off growl.

The hairs on Quinn's neck rose as he stood as still as possible.

Chester grinned. "That went well."

"That's good?" Quinn couldn't believe his voice actually squeaked.

"Oh, yeah. You don't want to know how Purrcevel reacts when he doesn't take a shine to you." Chester shuddered. "Well, I'll take the food to his bowl. You might want to follow me. I wouldn't stay in the room alone with him right now."

"What am I supposed to do when you leave?" Quinn hurried to keep up as they walked through the family room. What would he do with a cat the size of a mountain lion that obviously hated him? Maybe his aunt had left him the house and money because she *didn't* like him. Maybe living in the house for six months was a trial by fire.

Perhaps his aunt wanted him to attend church every week because he would be on his knees praying he wasn't attacked and eaten by a monster cat.

"Now, don't you worry," Chester said. "I'm sure you'll be fine. Just don't make eye contact."

Not sure if Chester snickered under his breath, Quinn tried not to glare at the man.

Chester stopped at the kitchen, which looked recently remodeled with top-of-the-line, light-gray cabinets and granite countertops. He spooned the food into a raised ceramic bowl, then checked what looked like a flowing cat water fountain. He tapped the spoon on the side of the dish, signaling the meal was ready.

He turned to Quinn. "Make sure you feed Sir Purrcevel breakfast and dinner. He has a snack for lunch. Also, keep checking his water. I wouldn't want to let him get too hungry or thirsty."

"I won't be staying here just yet. I have a reservation tonight at the hotel, and then I'm leaving in the morning to return to my apartment to get my belongings."

Chester gave him a quick nod. "Okay. You can take care of Sir Purrcevel until you leave." He opened a cabinet displaying food, treats, and cat toys. "Ms. Norma made sure he was well cared for, played with him every day, brushed his fur, and read to him before they went to bed at night."

"Read to the cat?" Quinn cut his eyes around the kitchen, looking for a hidden camera. This had to be a joke, or he'd entered an alternate universe.

"You might look on her nightstand in her bedroom. I'm not sure what they were reading together before she passed. Let me show you the rest of the house." Chester motioned him to follow. He stopped at the first open door. "This is the study."

Quinn was shocked. The room looked like something he would have furnished with steel and wood bookshelves, a modern desk, and a leather office chair. "The furniture looks brand new."

Chester nodded. "Norma had her whole house redone a few months ago and donated most of her original belongings to charity. She told my wife, Maybelline, she believed she would go home soon." He pointed upward. "Norma wanted everything ready for when you moved in. Let me show you the guest room."

Quinn walked to the next open door and stared at the bedroom outfitted with furniture and bedding again like something he would have purchased. How did his aunt know he would want the house and her inheritance? Had his mom talked to her?

Chester then led him to the master bedroom, again outfitted with new furniture. Even the bedding looked new. The house looked like it had been given a complete makeover in the style he would have chosen.

"Before Norma passed," Chester said. "She asked my wife to put all new, washed sheets and bedding in the bedrooms for you. Norma wanted to ensure you'd be comfortable when you moved into the house."

Quinn stepped to where a well-used Bible lay open on the nightstand. A sticky note with his name pointed to the highlighted verse of James 1:17: *Every good gift and every perfect gift is from above and comes down from the Father of lights, with whom there is no variation or shadow of turning.*

Why and how would his aunt know he would be here and see her Bible and that verse?

"I don't understand. I barely knew my aunt. Why would she prepare her house for me? How did she even know I'd be willing to come here?"

Chester rested his hand on Quinn's shoulder. "Son, your aunt has been praying for you for years. She knew you had lost your way but believed you'd get back on track with God, and everything would work out just fine."

Chapter 3

Quinn stood next to Chester on the front porch of his aunt's house.

"I've made up a list," Chester said as he handed Quinn a piece of paper. "This has my phone number, along with Henry Doss, who helps with Sirr Purrcevel, and Sammie Banks, who helped Norma with her yard work and odd jobs around her house. Make sure you contact all of us when you're leaving and when you'll return so we can take care of the cat and the yard. A group text is fine. Oh, and if you're hungry, Tiddlywinks restaurant downtown has great food."

"Thanks. I appreciate all your help."

"Call us anytime. I'm sure you and Sir Purrcevel will be just fine." He chuckled as he walked away.

Quinn rubbed his neck. His life sure had taken an interesting turn. He stood tall and tried to think positive thoughts. He could do this -- make friends with the cat and live in Crawdad Beach for six months.

He opened the door and spotted Sir Purrcevel lying on the couch, his amber eyes watching, probably plotting ways to kill him. Even though the cat wasn't growling, there was no way he would stay at the house alone. Quinn shuddered that he would have to sleep at the house when he returned.

Thankfully, the bedrooms did have locking doors. "Sir Purrcevel, I will be gone for a little while. Okay?" Quinn groaned at the absurdity of talking to a feline. The massive cat glared at him and flicked his tail in a whip of disdain.

Backing away, he locked the door behind him and sighed in relief. This afternoon, he would search the Internet for helpful hints on how to make a cat like him.

At least the day was a comfortable temperature. Quinn strolled down the quiet, tree-lined street. Most of the homes were older yet well-maintained. His mom would appreciate that most of the houses had flowers in planting beds or on their porches.

As he walked, Quinn called to update her and find out what she knew about the inheritance. She seemed as surprised as he was about the house since she hadn't talked to Norma other than a few times in the last few years.

How did his aunt know how to fix her house in ways he would like? Maybe he could check through Norma's bookshelves and see if there were photo albums or something that would give him hints of who his aunt was and how she knew anything about him.

A smiling, silver-haired gentleman with a little black and white dog walked on the sidewalk toward him. "Hello. You must be Quinn Young. I'm Henry Doss, and this is Filbert." He pointed at the little dog beside him, who wagged his tail in greeting.

Quinn shook the man's outstretched hand and patted the little dog's furry head. "Hello, nice to meet you and your pup."

"Welcome to Crawdad Beach," Henry said with a smile. "Are you heading downtown?"

"Yes, sir," Quinn said. "I'm going to try the restaurant."

"You'll enjoy their food." Henry kept in step beside him. "How did Sir Purrcevel treat you?"

"Well, he growled but didn't attack."

"He must like you. Chester should have given you my number. Don't hesitate to call anytime. Filbert and Sir Purrcevel are good friends."

"Really? A dog and a cat are buddies?"

"They are both intelligent and don't concern themselves with those who look different."

"Good for them," Quinn said. "It's a shame the rest of the world doesn't behave accordingly."

Henry smiled and nodded. "I agree. Will you be staying at your aunt's house tonight?"

"No, sir. I have a reservation at the hotel. I'll leave in the morning but return in a few days. It's odd that Aunt Norma wants me to stay in her home. I can't even figure out why she left me her estate. We weren't that close. I barely knew her."

"Your Aunt was a fascinating woman," Henry said. "She was part of the CBPT, which is the Crawdad Beach Prayer Team. Norma had an extraordinary relationship with the Lord. Without going into details, she requested prayer for you about eighteen months ago, and we've been praying for you ever since."

Quinn stopped and stared at the man. Why would his aunt have done that? How could she have known what was happening in his life then?

No *one* besides his co-workers should have known what happened eighteen months ago.

Paige surveyed her new home. The apartment was even nicer than the online photos, with a stone fireplace, brick walls, high ceilings, exposed beams and ductwork, an open and airy layout, and a kitchen with top-of-the-line appliances and granite countertops.

Large windows let in plenty of natural light, and French doors faced Main Street. She stepped onto the balcony that had enough room for a couple of chairs and potted plants. Most of the buildings on Main Street had flowers on their balconies. She'd make sure to do the same.

Paige returned inside. Her belongings were scheduled to arrive tomorrow, and she could start her new life. Since the clinic was only a few buildings away, maybe she'd get a pet to keep her company at night. Growing up, she'd had a variety of animals, including dogs, cats, beta fish, hamsters, and a bird that could talk.

Devin, her ex-boyfriend, had been allergic to anything furry. Now that she thought about it, he seemed allergic to anything that made her happy.

Paige groaned. Why had she put up with him all those years? Her family and friends had warned her, but for some crazy reason, she ignored everyone, even her own misgivings.

Why? She was an intelligent, college-educated woman with medical degrees. Why was she so lousy with love?

Those who tried to warn her thought Paige had clung to her boyfriend because of her fear of abandonment. Paige shook her head. Just because her dad had left, that didn't mean she had some phobia about men leaving. At least now she didn't need to worry about a man and could live her own life.

Paige locked up her apartment and trotted down the stairs. She'd eat at the little restaurant, then explore the shops around town.

Enticing smells lured Paige forward as she stepped inside Tiddlywinks restaurant. Even though it was crowded, she spotted a small table near the back.

She sat and picked up the menu, graced with a cartoon crawdad wearing a chef's hat. A cute brown-haired waitress wearing a peach short-sleeve polo shirt with an embroidered cartoon crawdad wearing a chef's hat on the pocket stopped by her table. "Hi, I'm Ursula. Are you ready to order?"

"Hi, Ursula. Have any recommendations?" Paige grinned at the young woman wearing a sparkling diamond engagement ring on her left hand.

"The food is always good. Today's special is homemade chicken tenders."

"Sounds good to me. I'll have that with green beans and mashed potatoes. And just a glass of water."

"Coming right up," Ursula said.

Paige watched the waitress stop at a table with the best-built, most handsome guy she'd ever seen. Ursula kissed the man before heading toward the back. The big guy watched her go like she was the most beautiful woman on earth. Paige let out a sigh.

Never in all the time she'd dated Devin had he looked at her like that. What a fool she'd been to stay with him. Maybe the first thing she needed to do was use the x-ray machine to have her head examined.

The restaurant door opened, and Paige noticed a nicely built, good-looking, well-tanned, curly, brown-haired guy about six feet tall step inside the restaurant. He glanced around the room, and his gaze rested on the empty table next to hers.

She wasn't in the market for a man, but Crawdad Beach sure did have excellent views.

Chapter 4

Even though the food was great, Quinn pushed aside his half-eaten lunch, paid his check, and left the restaurant. He'd noticed the great-looking woman with long, dark brown hair and big brown eyes sitting at the table beside him. Usually, he would have struck up a conversation, but instead, he'd ignored her. He didn't need to date anyone, not after what happened.

His mind a jumble of thoughts and regrets, Quinn walked the streets of Crawdad Beach. Eighteen months ago, his life had come apart when he'd been accused of theft by someone he thought loved him.

The claims against him were proven to be completely untrue when it was discovered that his fiancé was the one embezzling from the company. Quinn groaned and kicked a rock off the road.

His fiancé's father, a prominent businessman and politician, protected his daughter, ensuring all charges against her were dropped. Adding to the injustice, her father, with his fiancé's blessing, ensured Quinn's reputation was damaged.

Running away from things he couldn't change, he'd quit his job, moved out of the area, and chose a position where he could work from home.

Quinn stopped in front of his aunt's house. Since he had to stay here, he'd return to his apartment tomorrow morning and give notice. He'd sell or donate most of his possessions to make the move as easy as possible, especially since he liked most of the furniture in his aunt's house.

Once the six months were up and he received his entire inheritance, he'd take what he wanted from Norma's belongings, sell the house, and move wherever he desired -- somewhere far away where no one had ever heard of Quinn Young.

After lunch and checking into the hotel, Paige explored the downtown area. Since she loved prowling around antique stores, her first stop was Knick Knacks.

She stepped inside, and a bell over the door dinged. To her delight, the old building was crowded with antique and repurposed furniture, pictures, toys, glassware, and other items.

"Good morning." Carrying a stack of books, a young woman with long brunette hair walked toward her. "Can I help you find anything?"

"No, I'm just looking."

"My name's Grace if you need anything. Are you visiting our town?"

Paige instantly liked the young woman, who seemed about her age. "I'll be moving here. I'm with the new medical clinic."

"That's great. Welcome to Crawdad Beach. If you like to read, I have a new supply of books every week."

"I do enjoy reading." Paige followed Grace to a beautiful reading nook nestled among old, massive wooden shelves filled with books and decorative objects. Two chairs sat on either side of an old floor lamp.

"What do you like?" Grace asked as she arranged the book on a shelf.

"Mysteries, nothing gory or graphic, a touch of romance, and with humor."

Grace grinned as she handed her a novel. "I think you'll really enjoy this one. It made me laugh out loud and has a touch of mystery and romance. And, if you like that author, the library carries the rest of that series.

Paige read the back cover. "It does look interesting. I'll take it. Thanks."

The bell over the door dinged, and a tall, brown-haired, good-looking guy with a well-trimmed beard walked toward them. Without a word, he grabbed Grace and planted a big kiss on her lips.

Not sure what to do, Paige clutched the book against her chest as she stepped back to give them some privacy.

Grace giggled as she squirmed out of the man's embrace. "You nut. At least introduce yourself to our new resident."

The guy grinned at Paige. "Hi, I'm Jeremy. Please forgive my robust kiss with my wife. But we just learned this morning that she's pregnant with our first child."

Paige smiled at the couple. "Congratulations." She was genuinely happy for them, but a sharp pang of jealousy hit her.

"Thanks," Jeremy said as she put his arm around Grace, his gaze completely smitten. "We're excited."

"Paige will be working at the new medical clinic," Grace said as she gazed adoringly at her husband.

"I'm a nurse practitioner," Paige explained. "Dr. Abbott will be the main physician,"

"Great. Welcome to Crawdad Beach. Have you found a place to stay?"

Paige nodded. "I'll be downtown in the apartments."

"They are so nice," Grace said. "I lived in them with a roommate before I met Jeremy. I hope you'll like it here. We have a great church if you're looking for a place to worship. It's the white-steepled one as you came into town."

"Thanks. I noticed church when I drove into town." She hadn't attended church in a long time. For six years, her life had been wrapped up in pleasing a man instead of caring for herself or her relationship with God.

"No, pressure," Grace said. "We'd love to have you join us."

"The preaching is great, and we serve donuts and great coffee before the service," Jeremy added with a big grin. "Not that donuts and coffee are that important. Even though most days they are very appreciated."

"Thanks, I'll keep that in mind." Paige grinned as she held up the novel. "I'm ready to check out. I heard there's a nice trail by the river where I could read."

"Yes, you'll love it," Grace said as she led Paige to the check-out counter. "There are benches scattered along the trail where you can sit under the trees and enjoy the scenery and peace and quiet."

"Sounds like my kind of place." Paige paid for her purchase.

Grace finished the transaction and then handed her a business card. "My cell number is on the back if you need anything."

"Thank you, Grace. I appreciate that." Paige said goodbye and stepped out on the main street sidewalk. Living in Crawdad Beach was looking better by the moment.

With the book in hand, she walked to the end of the street, where the road curved around a community park. A historical marker revealed the town had been established in 1881 and received the name from one of the children who noticed a crawdad sunning himself on the small sandy riverbank. Now, the town's name made sense. She'd wondered why they weren't actually located on the beach.

Paige surveyed the park's blooming crepe myrtles, pine trees, a giant oak with moss hanging from its branches, and a play area for kids.

Fluffy white clouds floated in the blue sky as Paige walked the trail by the sandy river. A breeze stirred the leaves in the tree branches above her while the sounds of rippling water soothed and quieted her thoughts. Ignoring the benches, she spotted a nice place on the riverbank to sit.

Paige removed her shoes and placed her bare feet in the water. Seeing Jeremy and Grace together so happy and obviously in love and expecting their first child ignited a longing within Paige she'd tamped down for years.

Most of her friends were married with families of their own. Paige had stayed so busy with schooling, her career, and dating her jerk of an ex-boyfriend that she'd been isolated from people and God, letting life get away from her.

What if it was too late?

Chapter 5

"Here, kitty, kitty, kitty." Quinn set his laptop and suitcase on the floor and stood still, listening. Not a peep from the massive feline. He opened the curtains and let sunshine flood the room. Maybe he should try another tactic. "Sir Purrcevel, I'm here to live with you."

A low growl came from the hallway.

At the disturbing and non-welcoming sound, Quinn swallowed hard. There had to be a way to get the cat to like him. They were going to be roommates for the next six months. He'd already sold his furniture and closed out his apartment. Now that he'd be living here, he hoped the furry master of the house would accept him.

He needed to man up and show the cat who was in charge. Trying to act tougher than he felt, Quinn picked up his suitcases, walked to the spare bedroom, and laid them on the bed. Since the coast was clear, he returned to his car to retrieve the rest of his belongings.

After Quinn had unpacked his clothes, he removed the sack from his suitcase, which contained what he hoped would be the secret weapons for winning the feline's trust. He'd researched and purchased the best, most expensive, top-of-the-line catnip, toys, and treats.

Quinn went to the kitchen and opened Sir Purrcevel's cabinet. Thankfully, his food was well-stocked. He spooned out today's dinner and tapped the spoon on the side of the dish. "Sir Purrcevel, dinner is ready."

He waited five minutes before deciding it was time to take action. Taking his sack of cat goodies into the family room, he gave a healthy spritzing of catnip spray all over the furniture, the floor in front of the couch, and the new cat toys. He finished off by sprinkling catnip all over the floor. If that didn't make him a happy kitty, he didn't know what would.

Thirty minutes later, Quinn ran down the driveway as Chester sauntered toward him. "Hurry up! You've got to help."

Chester scoffed. "Just because you gave the cat a little catnip doesn't mean anything's wrong with him."

"You do *not* understand. Sir Purrcevel has gone bonkers. First, he rolled all over the floor, then the couch, and then he started running up and down the hall over and over again. Then he ran on top of the couch and lunged for me." Quinn shuddered. "He jumped into my arms and made the weirdest noise I've ever heard. Purrcevel gave a low, throaty purring noise as he looked right into my eyes like he either hated my guts or loved me, and I do mean *creepily* loved me."

Chester chuckled as he walked to the front porch and opened the door. "I'll take care of Sir Purrcevel for you."

Two minutes later, Chester screamed as he tore through the door. "He's gone mad!" He slammed the door behind him. "What did you do to that cat?"

Quinn grimaced. "I just spritzed some catnip around the room and on his toys and then sprinkled some of the catnip flakes around, too."

"How much did you use?" Chester leaned over as he tried to catch his breath.

Quinn shoved his hands into the pockets of his jeans. "A whole bottle of the spray and a packet of the flakes."

Chester grabbed him by the shoulders and shook him. "What were you thinking? It's a catastrophe."

"I was trying to be nice. I didn't want to hurt him. I just wanted him to like me."

"Okay. Let me think. Somebody has to know what to do." Chester took his cell phone from his back jeans pocket and searched the internet. "Since Purrcevel is so large, it looks like it won't cause him any long-lasting harm. He should be fine. I'm not sure when he'll act normal, though. I'll call Sir Purrcy's veterinarian to make sure."

Quinn sighed with relief. He never wanted to hurt an animal. Hopefully, the cat would be okay. He went back to the front porch and peered in the windows.

Sir Purrcevel spotted him from the couch and lunged toward the window.

Suspiciously eyeing Paige, the little blonde-haired girl clung to her mother.

Paige gave the girl a reassuring smile. "If I show you my

Band-Aid, will you show me your boo-boo?"

At a slight nod from the patient, Paige showed her the bandages the Abbots had made for their medical office.

The little girl's eyes widened as a look of pure delight crossed her pretty little face. "The crawdad!"

Paige chuckled. Treating the little girl was a breeze after she gave her the bandage. The idea of customizing them with a crawdad wearing a doctor's outfit had been a big hit with their young patients. Even some of their older patients had requested one.

After the little girl and her mom left, Paige entered her notes on the computer. A man's loud voice came from the waiting room. Rising to her feet, she peered down the hall.

With a mischievous expression, Nancy walked toward her. Following behind was an older gentleman and the nice-looking guy Paige had seen at the restaurant on her first day in town.

"Doc," the older man said. "You gotta help my friend. This is Quinn Young. He just moved here, and we had a cat incident."

Paige showed the men into the examining room. "A cat attacked you?"

The younger man grimaced as he cradled his arm. He sat on the exam table and gave her a sheepish look. "Kinda."

She didn't notice any scratches. "Can you tell me what happened?"

The older man stepped closer. "I'm Chester Taylor. Welcome to Crawdad Beach, Doc." He looked at her left hand, grinned at her, then at his friend. Chester cleared his throat as his expression turned serious. "Quinn was looking through the window, and the cat lunged for him. Quinn fell off the porch."

"I see." He was afraid of a little cat? Paige tried to keep a neutral expression as she turned to the cute guy. "Quinn, I'm going to examine you, okay?"

He nodded as his gaze went from hers to the floor. "It's probably nothing."

Paige gently probed his arm, feeling for any breaks. When she reached Quinn's elbow, he jerked and sucked in a breath. She motioned toward the door. "Let's get an X-ray. Chester, you can stay here or wait in the lobby."

"I'll stay here if you don't mind. I want to make sure Quinn's okay."

"That will be fine. Quinn, can you follow me, please?"

He nodded and walked next to her. "This is embarrassing."

"Accidents happen. It's part of life. Is Chester your dad?" She led Quinn into the X-ray room, had him sit, and helped him place his arm in the proper position.

"No, he's, I guess, a friend," Quinn said. "I met him last week. I just moved here."

"That was nice of him to help you. Try not to move." Paige stepped into the control room and took the image. "Okay, all done." Thankfully, with her many years of schooling, she had an X-ray technician degree.

Her friends said she was an overachiever, but she'd

wanted to be prepared for whatever job opportunities might arise. Paige took a minute to study the results before walking back toward him. "Nothing looks broken."

"That's good news," Quinn said. "I'm grateful there was a medical clinic close by. I appreciate all Chester's done helping me with the cat. He belonged to my great aunt. The cat, not Chester. My aunt passed away and left me her estate, which includes Sir Purrcevel."

"That's the cat's name?" Paige grinned.

Quinn smiled back at her. "He's a *big* cat."

"I love cats."

"You do?" Quinn followed her back down the hall. "Would you be willing to come to see him? He's acting strange."

She shook her head. "I'm not a veterinarian."

"I know, but you love cats, and I would really, *really* appreciate any help you could give."

"Let's take care of you first."

Chester met them at the exam room door. "How is he, Doc?"

"Nothing is broken." Paige waited until Quinn sat again on the exam table. "You're going to be sore and bruised. I'll put your arm in a sling to keep pressure off your elbow."

"Thank you. So, are you willing to check on Sir Purrcevel?"

"What a great idea," Chester said with a mischievous grin. "I called Sir Purrcy's veterinarian, and he assured me that since the cat is about the size of a mountain lion, he should be fine." He turned pleading eyes toward Paige. "But the poor kitty probably needs to be checked by a gentle hand."

"I'm not a veterinarian," Paige reminded them.

"We know that," Chester grinned. "but you're a doctor and a woman, and I'm sure Sir Purrcevel would appreciate your kind attention."

At Quinn and Chester's hopeful and desperate looks, Paige checked her watch. It was almost closing time. She did love cats, and getting to know Quinn might be an excellent way to end her day.

Chapter 6

"**I**'m excited you're going to help Quinn with his cat."

Paige shook her head at Nancy. "I'm a nurse practitioner, not a veterinarian."

Her friend handed Paige her purse. "True, but you've told me many times about how you used to doctor your pets when you were a little girl. Plus, Quinn needs you. He's cute, seems very nice, and based on his paperwork, he isn't married." She playfully shimmied her eyebrows.

"I'm not in the market for a man." However, she was curious about Quinn and the cat's situation.

"Wouldn't it be nice to have another friend in town? Someone close to your age? Actually, Quinn is the same age as you. I checked his paperwork. And you'll be able to get some kitty-loving. It's a win-win situation."

Paige sighed. "I'm going."

Nancy bounced on her toes. "I can't wait to hear what happens. I'll be praying."

"Are you going to pray about the cat or Quinn and me?"

Nancy grinned. "All the above." She wrapped her arms around Paige and hugged her tight. "We love you, and God loves you too."

Paige thanked her and went to her car. The Abbott's

belief in a loving God was sweet, but one Paige didn't understand. If God was loving, why did her dad leave? Why did her mom have to struggle as a single mother? Why did Paige date a loser? There were too many questions without answers.

A few minutes later, she parked her car at the address Quinn had given her and slid out of her seat.

The handsome, very anxious-looking man stood on the porch waiting for her. "I can't thank you enough for coming over."

"Not a problem. How's your elbow?"

"Sore, but okay." Quinn put his hand on the doorknob. "I'll go in first, okay?"

Paige tried not to roll her eyes. She'd never been around anyone with a fear of cats.

He stepped inside, waited for her to come in, then closed the door.

She glanced around the nicely decorated family room with a blue-gray sofa, two wingback chairs in the same color, and a wood coffee table. Light streamed in from the front window. Everything looked new, and the house seemed so peaceful.

"Sir Purrcevel," Quinn said. "I've brought someone to meet you." His gaze switched to her. "He's picky about how you greet him. Would you mind introducing yourself?"

Paige bit back her chuckle. "Are you serious?"

Quinn grimaced and shrugged. "Yeah, sorry. Do you mind?"

Paige couldn't believe she was going to formally address a cat. Not that she hadn't talked to her animals, but this was over the top. "Hello, Sir Purrcevel, my name is Paige Clark."

The loudest, meanest, deepest growl she'd ever heard came from the hallway. Paige gulped and moved behind Quinn. Thank goodness he had broad shoulders. "What kind of cat is he?"

He glanced over his shoulder. "Either a mountain lion or a combination of Bobcat and Persian."

Paige peeked over Quinn as the most gigantic cat she'd ever seen strolled toward them. He looked similar to a Maine Coon cat. However, the cat's face and ears resembled a bobcat with long gray fur like a Persian.

"At least he's not acting crazy anymore," Quinn said. "Hi, Sir Purrcevel. Sorry about giving you too much catnip. I was only trying to be your friend."

The cat jumped on the back of a wingback chair, narrowed his amber eyes at Quinn, and let out another hair-raising growl as his tail swished back and forth.

Quinn grinned her way, "I think he's forgiven me."

Paige gave a nervous chuckle. "You think so?"

He took a tentative step closer to the cat. "Could I pet you?"

The cat hissed.

Quinn stepped back and glanced at her. "Do you want to try? Maybe he'll like you better."

"Pet him?" Paige couldn't believe her voice shook. She took a deep breath. "Sir Purrcevel, could I pet you, please?"

The cat's tail stopped swishing as he surveyed her. Thankfully, he didn't growl. Maybe she'd be okay. "Sir Purrcevel, I'm going to pet your back, okay?" Paige gently stroked his surprisingly soft fur. His body tensed, then relaxed. A soft purr sounded from his throat.

"Aww, he's purring," Quinn whispered. "They said he hasn't purred since my aunt died."

"Poor thing. It's going to be okay now, Sir Purrcevel. Quinn will take good care of you."

The cat huffed out a breath as his attention jerked to Quinn.

Paige continued petting the animal, then nodded toward Quinn. "Maybe you could try to pet him with me."

At his touch, the purring stopped. Quinn groaned. "Aww, come on, Sir Purrcevel, would you give me a little purr?"

The cat's tail switched back and forth as he glared at Quinn. When he stepped away, the purring resumed. He sighed. "You sure do know how to hurt a guy's feelings. People have dissed me before, but this is the first time by a cat," he muttered.

Paige acted like she hadn't heard his comment, but his hurt was evident in the tone of his voice. "Quinn, why don't we move to the couch? Maybe he'll join us."

She took a seat as Quinn sat a cushion away. Paige turned to the cat. "Sir Purrcevel, if you'd like more petting, would you join us? Quinn seems like a pretty good guy. Your mom can't be with you anymore, so Quinn wants to take good care of you. Is that okay?"

The cat swished his tail as he glanced their way. After what seemed like forever, he jumped off the chair, meandered toward them, and, with a quick leap, settled between them and started purring.

Quinn's chocolate-brown eyes gave her an appreciative glance.

Between the soothing sound of Purrcevel's purr and feeling oddly comfortable with a man she just met, Paige leaned back and rested her head on the couch cushion.

Quinn couldn't believe Sir Purrcevel was purring and allowing him to pet his fur. He grinned at Paige. "Thank you. I really appreciate your help."

"My pleasure." She continued stroking the cat. "While I'm here, would you be willing to tell me about your aunt? Her house is very nice."

"I don't know that much about her. Norma was my great-aunt on my father's side. We weren't that close. Besides a few times as a kid, the last time I saw her was at my dad's funeral and then at my grandad's funeral. I had no idea she was leaving her estate to me. Chester said she'd even bought new furniture and upgraded her house before she passed. Almost like she knew what I liked."

"That is strange. Is that what brought you here?"

"Yeah, it's part of the stipulations in Norma's will. I have to live in her house, attend church, and take care of Sir

Purrcevel for six months."

"That was sweet of her to take care of you both."

Quinn pondered her statement. "I guess so. Did the new medical clinic bring you here?"

"Yes." Paige nodded. "Dr. Abbott and his wife are dear friends. I couldn't imagine staying in Charlotte without them. Other than time in college and medical school, Charlotte was home base. How about you?"

Feeling comfortable, Quinn stretched out his legs. "I moved here from Augusta, Georgia. Before that, I was in the Atlanta area. Since I work remotely, my computer is my office."

"That must be nice, but don't you feel isolated working online?"

"It's okay. Pays the bills. Interacting with people isn't always a good thing."

"That's true, but without meeting new people," Paige's brown eyes sparkled as she grinned his way, "you wouldn't have the delightful experience of sitting with a nurse practitioner petting a purring cat."

Quinn chuckled. "You've definitely given me a very nice, new experience."

He could identify with Sir Purrcevel because, sitting next to a beautiful woman, he felt like purring, too.

Chapter 7

The doorbell rang. Sir Purrcevel bolted upright, jumped from the couch, and ran to the front door.

Quinn shrugged at Paige as he walked over to see who was there. "I'm not sure who that could be. I'm not expecting anyone."

Holding what looked like food delivery bags, Chester and a woman with a bouffant hairdo stood on the porch. "We brought you dinner," Chester said.

"Come on in." Quinn stepped to the side to let them enter.

Sir Purrcevel was in full purr mode as he wrapped his tail around the lady's legs.

Chester turned to the woman standing next to him. "This is my wife, Maybelline." He glanced at Paige and gave Quinn a big smile. "Looks like everything went okay."

"We're sorry to bother you," Maybelline said. "Chester wanted to make sure things went okay with Sir Purrcevel. And I wanted to welcome you to Crawdad Beach. I cooked a few things for your dinner." She smiled at Paige. "There's enough for two."

Chester nudged his wife. "That's the new doc, Paige Clark."

"So, nice to meet you," Maybelline said. "We'll just take everything to the kitchen if that's okay?"

"Thank you. That's very nice of you," Quinn's stomach growled as he and Paige followed the couple into the kitchen.

Sir Purrcevel happily trotted next to Maybelline.

After placing the dishes on the kitchen counter, Maybelline scooped up the big cat and cuddled him. Sir Purrcevel purred so loud the dishes just about rattled as she baby-talked to him.

Quinn couldn't believe the shameless lovefest the cat was giving Maybelline.

Chester shrugged. "What can I say? My wife is a cat lover."

"Paige. Could I bring you a meal tomorrow?"

"You don't need to do that."

"It would be my pleasure and honor. We're glad you're here and thrilled about the new medical clinic."

"Thank you. I think I'm going to enjoy living here." Paige's gaze flitted toward Quinn.

He stood a little taller at her beautiful smile.

"Well," Maybelline said as she sat the cat down. "I think we better go." She took Chester's arm. "Call us if you need anything. And again, welcome to Crawdad Beach, you two."

After the couple left, Quinn turned to Paige. "I hope you'll stay and have dinner with me."

Paige grinned. "From the delicious smells coming from the dishes they brought, I wouldn't think of leaving."

Between dinner being the best meal Paige had eaten in ages and laughing at Quinn's fun stories, she couldn't remember a more entertaining evening.

After they ate, they sat in comfortable outdoor chairs on his back patio. Paige sipped lemonade as Quinn lit tiki torches to keep away the bugs. She hadn't been this relaxed in years.

Quinn was different from any other guy she'd met. He was manly yet sensitive, intelligent, handsome, and had a great sense of humor. He grew up in Hawaii and graduated from high school and college the same year she had. He didn't give a reason for moving from Atlanta to Augusta, but because he seemed uncomfortable talking about it, Paige wondered if he'd moved because of a bad relationship. She knew all about that subject.

Quinn took his seat next to her. "So, why did you move here?"

"I've worked with Dr. Abbott for years. When he wanted to open a satellite office, I couldn't see myself anywhere but with him. Even if it meant moving to a little town that enjoys cartoon crawdads."

He chuckled. "I guess neither of us thought we'd be living here. I'm glad we met. It's nice to have a friend to talk to."

"Likewise." Paige grinned at her new friend. "I'm sorry about your elbow, but not sorry you came to the office."

"Good thing you were there." Quinn's expression turned serious, but his eyes held a sparkle. "No telling what might have happened. My elbow could have permanently locked up, and my arm could have fallen off without proper care."

Paige laughed. "That's thinking the best-case scenario."

"Hey, you never know. If you hadn't come over, Sir Purrcevel might have clawed me to death in my sleep."

"Won't this be your first night alone in the house with him?"

Quinn's smile froze. "Thanks for reminding me."

"Sir Purrcevel is a good cat." She patted his arm. "You'll be fine."

"Easy for you to say. Did you know my aunt used to read to him before bedtime?"

"How sweet. What did she read? The Great Catsby? Animal Farm? A Tale of Two Kitties? Of Mice and Cats?"

"Ha ha ha. That was good. Now, I'll think of classic literature titles changed for cats all night. Chester told me that Aunt Norma used to read the Bible to Sir Purrcevel."

"The Bible? That's unusual."

Quinn leaned toward her. "And reading to a cat isn't?"

Paige puffed out a laugh. "True."

"You want to read to him?"

"Me? Why would I do that?"

"Because he likes you better," Quinn said with a grin.

Paige shook her head. Besides the strange thought of reading to a cat, she hadn't read the Bible in quite some time. "Sorry, but it's all on you."

Quinn sighed. "I can't believe you would say that to a wounded man." He cradled his arm and gave her a mischievous, pitiful look.

She nudged his foot. "Man up. You can handle it."

He grinned as he rubbed his leg as though she'd kicked him. "Man up? Is that what you say to your injured patients?"

"Only those who need a reminder."

Quinn raised an eyebrow as his gaze moved to her lips. "I'll be glad to man up."

Paige gulped as she tried not to look at his very kissable-looking mouth. A kiss from her handsome new friend would be very, very nice.

Chapter 8

Ready to kiss Paige's beautiful lips, Quinn leaned closer. A blur of fur hit the side of his face.

Sir Purrcevel landed on Paige's lap. Purring, the cat shot what looked like a smirk at Quinn.

Paige giggled as she stroked the cat's fur. "I didn't know you had a chaperone."

"Neither did I," Quinn muttered.

"How did he get out here anyway?"

"That is a good question and a very disturbing thought that he can escape."

"We had a cat that used his paws to open paddle-type doorknobs."

"That's how he did it." Quinn gave a playful glare at Sir Purrcevel and made a mental note to see how many doorknobs needed replacing in the house. First thing in the morning, he would visit Doohickeys Hardware.

"I guess I better get home." Paige waited until the cat jumped off her lap and then stood. "I had a very nice evening."

"I did, too." Quinn followed her through the house and outside. "Thanks again for coming over and helping me with Sir Purrcevel."

In the moonlight, Paige leaned against her car. "I didn't

do much."

Quinn brushed his hand over Paige's soft cheek. "You helped me in more ways than you know, and you helped a cat find his purr." Lowering his face to hers, he kissed Paige's sweet lips.

A soft moan came from her throat as her arms wrapped around him, drawing him closer.

She shouldn't be kissing him. Her wounded, cautious heart was screaming for her to stop, but the yearning inside wanted to love and be loved, to be in the arms of someone who cared.

But this wasn't love. She barely knew Quinn and didn't even know if he cared.

Paige pushed out of his embrace. "I'm sorry. I shouldn't have kissed you."

"Kissed me? I thought I was the one who initiated contact."

She couldn't help but giggle. "Initiate contact?"

Quinn rubbed a hand over his face. "Sorry, that didn't sound very romantic. You're a *great* kisser. Okay, that didn't sound very suave either." He shoved his hands into his back jeans pocket. "I've basically been sitting in front of a computer for eighteen months and haven't gotten out much." He groaned and rubbed his forehead as though what he shared was a mistake.

Paige laid her hand on his arm. "I wouldn't have guessed you've been keeping to yourself. I enjoyed talking to you and very much enjoyed your contact initiation."

Quinn grinned as he leaned next to her against the car. "Thanks. I hope you'll forgive me if I came on too strong since we just met."

"It's not like we're kids anymore."

"True. And you're my healthcare professional. So, doc, are my lips working okay?"

Paige laughed as her cheeks heated. "Oh, yes. I think your lips are just fine. I better go." She opened her car door and slid into her seat.

Quinn gazed down at her. "Thanks for a great evening. But I will probably need more help with Sir Purrcevel. No telling how he will act tomorrow." He took out his phone. "Could I have your number?"

"You probably will need additional help." She shared the information with him and got his.

"Thanks, Paige." His grin showed his dimple. "I'm glad you're here in town."

"I'm glad you're here too."

Paige returned to her apartment and sat on the edge of her couch. Why had she felt so comfortable with Quinn, and why had she kissed him?

They had many things in common. They liked the same music and even had the same favorite movies. Maybe she let her guard down because there were no expectations; only two people were trying to care for a lonely cat. Wasn't it?

Paige sighed. She knew better. It was her heart that was lonely. She groaned as she looked around her apartment. Her furnishings were sparse and well-worn. She could now afford better things but had spent most of her money to pay off her school loans or buy Devin gifts. Any shopping they did together was for his house, his clothes, and whatever *he* wanted to buy. When they went on dates, Devin chose the restaurants, movies, and even the vacations they took together. Everything hinged around what he liked and making his life better.

What a fool she'd been to spend years trying to please Devin, doing anything and everything he wanted, anything to make him stay, anything to make him happy. She'd lost her friends and barely kept in touch with her mom while she dated him because Devin said he wanted her all to himself. What a lie. He isolated her so she wouldn't see how she was being manipulated and used.

She'd taken nothing from the relationship because there was nothing to take. Six years wasted. If she didn't have her job, she would have anything. Why, oh why, had she stayed with Devin?

Paige shoved off the couch, went to her bedroom, changed her clothes, and crawled into bed.

On top of her dresser stood the small stuffed bear her dad had given her on her twelfth birthday, only a few days before he left. Her mom had remarried, moved on with her life, and was happy with a man who treated her like a princess. Paige sighed. Why couldn't she?

Instead, she kept reliving her desperate cries as her father drove away, leaving her screaming and shivering in the middle of a thunderstorm.

Chapter 9

Finishing his work assignment, Quinn stood and rubbed his computer-tired eyes. His back ached from sitting too long, and he needed to stretch his legs. Tomorrow, he'd order a standing desk to make his life easier.

Quinn went to the kitchen for a drink of water and leaned against the counter. Yesterday's time with Paige had been outstanding. Besides being a cat-whisperer, she was gorgeous and intelligent, had a great sense of humor, and was a terrific kisser.

But why would someone like her want to get involved with him? He'd like a friend, but between his past and the fact he was leaving in a few months, what was the use of pursuing a relationship?

Finishing his drink, he walked down the hall, stopped, and flipped on the light in the master bedroom. His aunt's Bible remained open. He stepped closer. How could it be on another page?

Another sticky note with his name pointed to the verses in Isaiah 43:18-19: *Do not remember the former things, nor consider the things of old. Behold, I will do a new thing, now it shall spring forth; shall you not know it? I will even make a road in the wilderness and rivers in the desert.*

Quinn gulped. A date written beside the highlighted verses was the day he lost his job eighteen months ago. No one besides the people he worked with should have that information. How would his aunt know? And how did the Bible's pages get flipped?

Sir Purrcevel jumped onto the bed next to him and stared.

In jest, Quinn addressed the cat. "Did you turn the pages?"

The cat seemed to taunt him with a loud meow.

"You're kidding. You didn't do this, did you?"

Sir Purrcevel purred.

"You're purring? Seriously, this is some kind of joke." Quinn looked up at the ceiling. "Right?"

What was he doing addressing God? He didn't have any right to talk to God, not when he was the one who walked away.

His parents were committed Christians, sweet people who loved God, and kept Quinn active in church since he was a baby. Even in college and afterward, he'd attended services. He hadn't been perfect but tried to live a good life . . . until his life exploded.

Quinn glared at the ceiling. How could God allow false accusations to be made against him by a woman who he thought he'd marry? Why didn't God intervene and take care of him? Why did he lose his job when people wrongly believed he was a thief?

Nothing was fair about what happened. Quinn stomped back to his office, slumped in his chair, and raked his hands through his hair.

Why and how could an elderly aunt who barely knew him leave highlighted verses in her Bible for him to read? It was creepy, otherworldly, and disturbing. Or was his aunt's inheritance and the verses she left for him divinely orchestrated?

Quinn's skin pebbled. He'd read the Bible and heard stories of people who had God encounters, but why would God want anything to do with him?

But what if it was real and the verses were God reaching out to him? The first verse his aunt left for him was about good and perfect gifts coming down from God. Quinn scratched his chin. He couldn't deny that an unexpected inheritance was a very good gift. The next verses were about God doing new things. He'd sure like some good, new things in his life.

Maybe it was time to start talking to God again because it did seem like God might be trying to get his attention.

The clinic closed for the day; Paige reviewed her notes as she walked toward her office.

Nancy came beside her, keeping pace. "I've been meaning to ask you all day. How was your evening last night with Quinn and his cat?"

Paige tried to hide her grin as she shrugged. "It went well. I think Sir Purrcevel just needed a feminine touch."

Nancy snorted a laugh. "Sir Purrcevel? That's the cat's name?"

"Yes, but he's not just a cat. He's a *massive* animal." Paige held out her hands. "He's bigger than those Maine cats or a Lynx. Sir Purrcevel's parents were probably a Persian and a Bobcat or a cross between a Maine cat, Lynx, or maybe a Bobcat." Paige sat at her office desk.

Nancy's eyebrows raised as she sat in the chair facing her. "That sounds like a mountain lion. But you still didn't tell me about your evening with Quinn."

"It was successful. Thankfully, Sir Purrcevel is super sweet once he gets to know you."

"So, was your evening successful because of a cat or his handsome owner?"

"Quinn is a very nice guy." Probably the nicest she'd met in years. Plus, he was handsome and fun.

"Good. You deserve to be around nice men."

Not with all her mistakes. Paige pretended to read a file on her desk. "I don't know about deserving anything."

"Oh, Paige. Stop selling yourself short. You're a beautiful, intelligent, sweet young woman. It's time for you to enjoy life."

"I enjoy life." *Didn't she?*

"In some ways. You enjoy your work and your patients, but your personal life has been, well, let's just say, extremely lacking. Devin never treated you right. Please, find a nice guy who treats you like a princess."

"Princess? You've read too many fairy tales."

Nancy tapped the desk. "Fairy tales usually contain difficulties, and you've had your share, but that doesn't mean you shouldn't look for someone who wants the best for you."

"That would be nice, but maybe it's too late." She was in her thirties and never married because she wasted years in a lousy relationship.

"Oh, good grief." Nancy made a pfft sound. "I have friends who didn't get married until they were much older than you. I've heard several people in this town married for the first time when they were in their sixties."

Paige slumped in her chair. "If I have to wait another thirty years, what's the use?"

"Don't give up. I believe this is your year for something amazing to happen in your life."

"Well, if not, you owe me a big steak dinner at the end of the year."

Nancy stood and held out her hand. "Shake on it, and the deal is made."

Chapter 10

"**I** hope we didn't come too early. Filbert wants to play with Sir Purrcevel. They've been friends for years, and I'm afraid Filbert has been rather depressed the last several days since we haven't been over to visit." With an apologetic look, Henry stood on Quinn's front porch with his little dog.

Meowing like crazy, Sir Purrcevel ran to his dog friend and rubbed against him.

"Well, what do you know." Quinn chuckled. "They really do like one another." He moved aside to let Henry and the animals inside. "I thought dogs and cats were enemies."

"In some cases, yes." Henry sat on the couch as the animals played chase. The man's kind blue eyes gazed his way. "How are you settling in?"

Quinn sat in the wingback chair across from Henry. "I'm doing okay. I have a remote job, so continuing my work was no problem."

"I know your aunt would be pleased that you're here." Henry gazed around the room. "She was a special woman who loved the Lord."

"I can believe that. Aunt Norma left highlighted Bible verses for me in her Bible. How could she know I would be willing to come here? She even seemed to know things I've never shared with anyone."

"Your aunt spent her days reading the Bible and praying," Henry said. "She was the happiest, most contented person I've ever met, gifted in many ways, encouraging, comforting, and helping others. I believe her affection and concern for you came from her close walk with God."

With a big meow, Sir Purrcevel vaulted to the top of Quinn's chair, almost tipping them over. The cat then jumped in front of Filbert. The little dog yipped and ran from the room with the cat on his heels.

Quinn shook his head. "That is the weirdest thing I've ever seen."

The cat came tearing back into the room, followed by Filbert. Their barks and meows sounded like laughter as they weaved around the furniture and ran down the hall.

Quinn sat back in his chair and glanced at Henry. "Do you really think Norma knew things about me because she was close to God? Would God do things like that? I mean today, not just like we read in the Bible." He couldn't believe he was having a conversation like this, but he felt comfortable with the man. Henry reminded him of his late grandfather.

"The Lord moves in mysterious ways," Henry said with a gentle smile. "Every day, God is working and moving, touching lives, guiding, directing, and helping us through our journeys. He often places people on our hearts to pray for them or reach out in person. God is not limited to the times of the Bible."

"I thought God had abandoned me." The words slipped

out and hung in the air.

Henry's head tilted as he surveyed him. "Norma leaving you her inheritance, and the verses she left prove that God's love never left you. However, even if you didn't see or feel anything, God's love was and is always present."

"I needed God's help eighteen months ago." Quinn shoved out of his chair and walked to the front window. He did appreciate what his aunt had done for him, but where was God when he'd been falsely accused, when he lost the woman he loved, when he lost his friends, his job, and everything that mattered to him?

Henry came next to him. "God's timing isn't usually on our schedule, and difficulties touch us all. Even God's Son, Jesus Christ, suffered in ways we can't imagine. Yet, there is always a greater plan and purpose than we can see."

"Why doesn't God show us, help us, promise it will be okay? It's like I was walking along doing just fine, and someone pulled the rug out from under me and kicked me when I was down."

"I'm sorry for your pain." Henry's words were genuine, kind, and compassionate.

"Thanks. Not your fault. I grew up in church, heard all about God's love, and I loved Him too, but then when things got tough, God left me."

Henry's kind gaze settled on Quinn. "Do you believe God left you, or did you leave God?"

Quinn stiffened, then groaned. "Maybe both."

"Have you asked God about the situation?" Henry asked.

"I don't know. I got angry. Yelled, kicked, threw a few things, busted a chair, went to the gym to lift weights until I pulled a muscle, broke a toe when I kicked the wall, and then I moved out of the area."

Henry grimaced. "Those activities don't sound very helpful. May I make a suggestion?"

Quinn shrugged. "Sure."

"Take your Bible, a piece of paper, and a pen, sit quietly and talk to God. Ask Him every question you have, tell God everything that hurt and disappointed you, then listen and write down everything you hear."

Quinn scoffed. "I'll probably hear my thoughts rampaging through my head."

"You might be surprised if you take time to really listen. In the verse Jeremiah 33:3, God says to call to Him, and He will tell you great and mighty things you do not know. Our Heavenly Father wants to hear from His children to provide love, guidance, comfort, and wisdom. "

Quinn stared out the window. He'd asked God many questions about what happened but never expected an answer. He'd read the Biblical accounts of God talking to people, but that was then.

Tails dragging and panting, Filbert and Sir Purrcevel walked into the room and collapsed.

"Looks like it's time for us to go," Henry said. "Thank you for allowing us to interrupt your morning."

"I'm glad you came over. Thanks for talking to me."

"My pleasure." Henry laid his hand on Quinn's shoulder.

"Call anytime. And, if it's not too big an imposition, could Filbert and I visit every few days?"

"Both Sir Purrcevel and I would enjoy the company."

After they left, Quinn remained rooted to the floor in front of the window while a contentedly purring Sir Purrcevel lay on the floor.

Could Henry be right? If Quinn asked God direct questions and sat quietly, would he hear something besides his own thoughts?

Maybe it was time to find out the truth.

While a young mom anxiously watched from the side of the exam table, Paige listened to the little girl's heart and lungs. Thankfully, the little one's cold hadn't settled in her chest.

The door to the exam room opened, and a young man rushed to where the little girl was sitting.

"Daddy, you came!" She vaulted into his arms.

Her father kissed her forehead as he hugged her tight. "I'll always be here for you."

After the family left, Paige closed her office door and pressed her back against the wall. Emotion clogged her throat as she fisted her hand over her mouth. She never had a daddy who was there for her, a father who cared. Why did those facts still hurt and haunt her?

"Paige?" Nancy's voice came from the hallway. "Are you

alright?"

Paige straightened. "I'm fine. I'll be right there." She grabbed a piece of paper off her desk and opened the door. "I forgot this."

Nancy glanced at what Paige had in her hand and scrunched up her nose. "You forgot that?"

"Well, I thought maybe I needed to take a second look."

Nancy chuckled. "Well, you just go ahead and check the invoice for toilet paper and bathroom essentials."

Heat rocketed up Paige's back. "Okay, fine. I just needed a minute." She shoved the paper into her scrubs pocket.

Nancy stepped beside her. "Want to share what's bothering you?"

"We don't have time." Paige tried to maneuver around her friend. "Isn't there another patient waiting?"

"Nope. Just you and me. We are closed for lunch, and Adam is out running an errand. What's going on?"

Paige crossed back to her desk and collapsed in her chair. "Our last patient was a little girl with a super sweet dad, and all I could think about was how rotten my dad had been. I'm a grown woman. Why does that keep bothering me?"

"I'm sorry." Nancy sat across from her. "There are some things on this side of heaven that I don't think will ever make sense."

"It's ridiculous that I'm upset about seeing a loving father. I should be thrilled that the little girl has a good dad. Adam is probably a wonderful father, isn't he?"

"Yes, he is." Nancy nodded. "I'm blessed with a loving

husband, and our children have a loving and caring father. But Paige, Adam came from a horrible family. He'd been abused in terrible ways."

"What?" Paige felt like she'd been punched in the stomach. How was that possible? Adam Abbott was the kindest, gentle man she'd ever known. "Why didn't I know that? How did he turn out to be such a nice man?"

"God is good about making masterpieces out of messes. After graduating high school, Adam joined the army to escape from his abusive parents. He received his degrees through service in the medical corps. After that, he went into private practice. Along the way, God provided Christian men who pointed Adam to a loving heavenly Father. No matter how flawed or good an earthly dad might be, we have a perfect, loving Heavenly Father."

"I'm grateful that Adam was able to get over his past. But that just makes me feel even worse that I'm complaining about my dad."

"Oh, please don't think that way," Nancy, her gaze compassionate, leaned toward her. "Adam often reminds me that once we've been through something, we need to remember we went *through* it. We don't have to stay there anymore. It's okay to grieve what was lost, and moments of sadness are part of life, but please don't miss the new mercies and opportunities God gives each day. Don't miss what is ahead by focusing on what was behind. You've been through difficulties and made it to the other side. You're a survivor."

Paige considered Nancy's statement about being a

survivor. Maybe that was true, but still, she struggled with disappointment with her father and the deep regrets of the years she spent with Devin.

Nancy sat back in her chair. "Do you remember the man you treated a few years ago who'd tried for a month to take care of a deep cut on his leg by himself?"

"Yes, that was bad. The poor man's methods of self-medication did not work, plus he kept picking at the sore, making his wound even worse." Paige's stomach churned a touch at that memory. The guy had almost waited too late to seek help. "

Nancy's gentle gaze met hers. "He should have called for help and allowed treatment because deep wounds heal from the inside out. God is the Great Physician. Paige, please take your soul wounds to Him. He is the one who heals the broken-hearted and binds up wounds."

Chapter 11

Her work over for the day, Paige walked on the trail beside the river. A light breeze blew the tree leaves, making dappled shadows along the trail. With all her medical training, why wasn't she more intelligent in dealing with her own deep wounds?

The rhythmic sound of a jogger came from behind her. "Passing on your left," the woman's voice said.

Paige moved to the right and waited.

A young woman with a lightning bolt shaved in her dark hair came beside her and continued jogging in place. "You're the new doctor in town, right?"

"I'm the nurse practitioner." Paige grinned at the woman who looked about her age.

"Same thing." She waved a dismissive hand. "You have the training and smarts of a doctor. By the way, my name's Alexa. Welcome to Crawdad Beach."

"Thanks, Alexa. It's nice to meet you. I'm Paige Clark."

"Good to meet you, Paige. It's great to have a medical clinic in town. I'll see you around." Alexa grinned and zipped away.

Paige chuckled. Seeing that Alexa ran as fast as lightning, her hair design made sense.

Settling on a bench facing the river, Paige leaned forward, propped her elbows on her knees, and placed her chin in her hands. Had she been running away from God instead of running to Him?

The sun sparkled like diamonds on top of the water as the river flowed unhindered, moving forward. Why couldn't she live like that and let life flow?

If only she could leave behind the issues with her father and her wasted years with Devin. Her mom had talked to Paige many times, telling her that forgiveness was the key to releasing the past. Her mom refused to live in bitterness and had forgiven Paige's dad. Mom now had a great new life with a man she loved and who loved her.

Paige sighed. So, if she was going to do this, she needed to go to God, the Great Physician, and forgive others, forgive herself, release everything to God, let go, move on, look forward instead of back, and embrace the new. Good grief, she couldn't do any of those things on her own. She'd tried for years.

She rose to her feet and continued walking on the trail. Devin had used her for years. Why had she chosen to stay with him? For six years, she'd been uncomfortably comfortable in the relationship, allowing her insecurity and feelings of abandonment by her dad to rule her actions and emotions.

Paige kicked at a rock on the trail. She'd been such a fool. Glancing at the water, she stopped when she noticed debris clogging against the riverbank.

Kneeling, Paige removed the sticks and old leaves until the water ran free. Sitting back, she looked up at the sky. Oh, how she wanted to be free. "God, help me, please."

Quinn spent time praying and reading the accounts in Genesis about Joseph. The poor guy was sold into slavery by his brothers, falsely accused by his employer's wife, and spent years in prison. But then God orchestrated his freedom to become Egypt's second highest-ranking ruler to save the Egyptian people and Joseph's family from famine. Years later, when he was reunited with his brothers, he told them that what they meant for evil, God used for good.

Quinn flipped to Romans 8:28 and read; *all things work together for the good of those who love God and are called according to His purpose*. All things? Wait, didn't Jesus say all things are possible for God?

"Did you know about all of this?" Quinn read the Bible verses out loud again and then glanced at Sir Purrcevel lying beside him on the couch. "I bet Aunt Norma read you these, didn't she?"

The cat gave a contented purr.

Quinn grinned. They had become best buds since he'd been reading to Sir Purrcevel. "Don't tell anyone about me talking to you, okay? I don't want people to think I'm crazy.". Maybe he was off his rocker since he was reading Bible verses and discussing what he'd found with a cat.

Obviously, he spent way too much time alone. Well, regardless of what the cat or other people thought, he had an incredible time with God, getting answers to his many questions.

Quinn bowed his head in prayer, giving God all his disappointment, hurt, and anger at what happened. As he prayed, a surprising peace covered his shoulders.

Even though what happened still stung, he realized he'd been rescued from a relationship that would have been a long-term nightmare. His ex-fiancé had used and manipulated him for her sordid purpose to gain access to the company account information. He'd been an idiot to trust her.

Now, he understood that if the relationship had gone further, there was no telling what might have happened. God did and *would* work good things in his life.

Closing the Bible, Quinn said a prayer of thanks. For the first time in a long time, he felt free from his past and had hope for the future.

It was time to look for new ways to enjoy his new life. Quinn grabbed his phone and placed the call.

Chapter 12

A golden peach sunset above them, Paige stayed beside Quinn as they walked along the beach. A group of teenagers played in the water, splashing and teasing one another. The ocean water was as far as could be seen, the sun glinting off the waves.

Paige sidestepped two seagulls fighting over a scrap of food and glanced at Quinn. "Thanks for dinner. It's been way too long since I had fresh seafood."

Looking quite handsome in his khakis and polo shirt that showed his trim but muscular body, Quinn grinned her way. "I'm grateful you didn't mind me contacting you with such short notice."

"Not at all. Your timing was perfect." She'd just finished a shower when he called and had no plans other than to lie on her couch and read.

"You mentioned you walked the trail after work. I haven't been there yet. Is it worth visiting?"

"Yes, it's great for walking, running, sitting on a bench reading, or watching the lazy river." Paige smiled at the memory of her quiet moment with God.

"Since you're smiling, it must be nice. I'll have to try it soon."

"I think you'll like it," Paige said. "Do you jog or run?"

Quinn shrugged. "Not much anymore. I was on the track team in high school and college."

"I'm impressed. Have you seen Alexa?"

Quinn raised an eyebrow. "The computer voice?"

Paige chuckled. "No, Alexa lives in town. She has a lightning bolt shaved in her black hair."

"I heard there was a big-time track star living in town. I haven't met her yet. Guess I need to get out more often."

"I've only visited a few places too. Maybe we can explore together."

Quinn's dimple showed with his grin. "I'd like that."

"So, were you a fast runner in school?"

"I was pretty good and won a few awards, but I was never like lightning. How about you? Were you involved in athletics?"

"Not at all. I was a mutant nerd interested in science."

Quinn stopped. "I don't believe you were ever anything but beautiful."

Heat igniting her back, Paige dipped her head and stared at the sand beneath her feet. "Thank you for your kind words, but I have photo proof of my less-than-attractive years. Before I had eye surgery, my glasses were as thick as the bottom of pop bottles, and I was so skinny the kids at school said if I turned sideways, I would disappear."

He tipped her head up to look at him, his chocolate-brown eyes searching hers. "Paige, whatever you were or however you saw yourself, you are *not* that way now. You're incredibly gorgeous."

Her eyes misting, Paige bit her lip to stop it from trembling. Quinn thought she was gorgeous? Devin never told her she was pretty unless he wanted something physical.

Quinn swept a strand of hair off her face. "You don't believe me? You really are beautiful."

Paige turned away, faced the ocean, and crossed her arms over her chest. How could she believe Quinn? Her father didn't want her, and for six years, she tried to please a man who walked out on her.

Seeing the vulnerability in her expression, Quinn stepped beside Paige. How did she not know how beautiful she was?

How could he help her understand? Something from his own experience might help. "When my sister was a little girl, she fell off her bike. Not just fell but face-planted on concrete. Blood was everywhere."

Paige sucked in a breath and glanced in his direction. "Was she okay?"

"She was fine, but her chin took the brunt of her fall, which left a big scar. For years, she refused to believe she was pretty. Every time she looked in the mirror, all she noticed was her scar." Quinn moved in front of Paige and ran his fingers along her soft cheek. "My sister is a beautiful woman, but no matter how many times people told her she was beautiful, she still wouldn't believe it."

"A few years ago," Quinn continued, "my sister married a man who adores her and sees her beauty. One day, my sister's little girl ran her tiny fingers along my sister's scar. With the innocence of a child, she asked why she couldn't have a beauty mark like her beautiful momma."

He gently cupped Paige's chin in his hand and pivoted her head his way. "I don't know who has left a scar on how you see yourself, but Paige, inside and out, you're a beautiful woman."

Paige's eyes shimmered with unshed tears. "Thank you." Her voice was only a whisper.

Quinn kissed her trembling lips, took her in his arms, and held her close. They were only friends, but for some strange reason, he felt he'd known her for years.

She couldn't remember a time Devin had told her she was beautiful. Clinging to Quinn's strong embrace, Paige let her tears fall. It wasn't a snot-producing, full-out cry but more of a gentle cleansing release. In Quinn's arms, she felt safe as her heart kept in time with his steady heartbeat.

Paige drew in a deep breath to wrestle back her tears. "Sorry about that." She stepped out of Quinn's embrace and wiped her face. "I got your shirt wet, too. I'm so sorry."

"Don't be. Guys need hugs, too, you know. As my friend and medical professional, you provided me a much-needed service."

Paige frowned as she waved her hand between them. "Is that what this is?"

"No, it's more of an advanced friendship."

"Advanced?" Paige's back stiffened.

He grinned with a nod. "Yes, kisses and hugs are part of the advanced friendship package."

Paige's stomach churned. How far did Quinn think their friendship would go? She shook her head. "I'm *not* in for a friends-with-benefits thing." She had enough mistakes and regrets.

"Wait, no. I'm not either." Quinn's eyes went wide as he held up his hands. "I've been burned before and am not rushing into any relationship. And I do *not* take advantage of my friends." He looked away. "Not like some people," he muttered.

Paige studied him, wondering about his past relationships and how their friendship would work. "Aren't you planning on leaving in a few months?"

"I'm not sure about that. I'm enjoying living in Crawdad Beach. The house is nice, and Sir Purrcevel does *not* need another loss in his life. How could I leave?" He took her hand in his. "I might just stay for the long haul."

Paige held up their joined hands. "Is this part of the advanced friendship?"

His eyes sparkling, he gave her a quick nod. "Definitely. Friendly, but not too friendly." He kept hold of her hand as he led her along the shoreline. "I'm just making sure you don't trip or fall."

She puffed out a chuckle. "Right. A grain of sand might catch my foot."

"It is a hazard. Plus, there are sand crabs, attacking seagulls, clueless teenagers running amok, flying beach balls, and many other dangers." He shuddered. "As a gentleman, I want to protect my beautiful friend."

Paige stared at Quinn. "I've never been around anyone like you."

"I'll take that as a compliment and not an insult." He stopped, his gaze searching hers. "I haven't had a friendship like this either. I have no idea why I feel comfortable with you. Maybe because you saved me from certain death at the claws of Sir Purrcevel."

Paige laughed. "Is that what this is?"

"I don't know." He shrugged his shoulder. "But I hope you're enjoying being with me as much as I am with you."

She squeezed his fingers and met his gaze. "I am very much enjoying being with you."

His smile spread. "Thanks, friend. What do you say we get some ice cream before heading back to Crawdad Beach?"

"I think you are a very wise friend."

After a wonderful evening of talking and laughing, Quinn kissed her goodnight with a sweet, lovely kiss.

Inside her apartment, Paige collapsed on her apartment couch. She couldn't remember a more enjoyable time. There were no awkward moments or the fear of saying or doing something that would offend or upset him; it was just an easy friendship.

She'd laughed more with Quinn than she had in years. Could they continue a friendship like they had started? She rubbed her finger across her lips. Quinn's kisses were gentle, not demanding or pushy. They were sweet and kind. Why didn't anyone tell her guys could be so nice?

What a fool she'd been. Devin's kisses had been forceful and demanding, driven out of passion to suit his own needs. Paige groaned at the memory as she shoved off the couch and paced in her den.

At least now she had the opportunity to spend time with a nice guy. Then again, Devin had been a gentleman for the first month.

She needed to keep her guard up and not get too close to Quinn.

But if she did that, what would she miss?

Chapter 13

While Dr. Abbott cared for the last patient, Paige hurried to her office. She'd been in what Quinn termed an advanced friendship for two months.

They'd been with one another every evening, spent Saturdays together, and even attended church on Sunday mornings. Quinn had explained it was part of the stipulations in his aunt's will, but Paige watched him and could tell he enjoyed being there. He even took notes. She had to admit she also liked the services.

Their friendship was more of a best friend type thing than a dating relationship. She and Quinn watched old movies on television, played board games, spent hours talking, or hung out at the beach. Most people would probably think it strange that the physical part of the relationship never went beyond kissing. That didn't mean Paige wasn't finding it more challenging to avoid crossing the line of a sweet friendship.

Curious to see what Quinn had texted, Paige checked her phone. She grimaced as she stared at a text from Devin's best friend, Clancy. The man now thought she would be available to date him. Ugh. Never in a million, zillion years would she want anything to do with him. The man was obnoxious and slimy. Thank goodness he didn't live near her anymore.

Paige deleted Clancy's text, then grinned at the cute photo Quinn had sent her of Sir Purrcevel lying across his office desk. Poor Quinn barely had room for his keyboard. His text read, *Help! Being held hostage. Save, please!*

She sent him a quick reply that she'd come to his rescue at 5:30.

"Do you have any plans this evening?" Nancy grinned as she stood in the doorway.

"You know I do." Paige smiled at her friend. "Quinn needs rescuing from Sir Purrcevel."

"I'm sure he does." Nancy chuckled. "From your walking on-air attitude, I'd say things are going well. Especially since you two spend every non-working hour together, and he's sent you roses twice in the last two weeks, your friendship seems to be progressing."

"We're just friends." Paige turned off her computer. "I didn't know friendship with a man could be so enjoyable."

"I'm happy for you. I like Quinn. What does he do for a living?"

"He's an Investment Banking Analyst. I was surprised he could work from home. He tried to explain what he did, but it was over my head." Paige took her purse from her desk drawer and placed the strap over her shoulder.

Nancy followed her down the stairs. "By the way, I've hired a receptionist to help us around the office—her name's Ursula. Maybe you've seen her working at Tiddlywinks Restaurant. She'll continue waitressing in the morning, then come in to help for a few hours in the afternoon."

"I've met her," Paige grinned. "She's adorable. Isn't she engaged to Valentino?" Ursula was a beautiful young woman, but her fiancé could be an action hero in the movies with his dark hair and dark-brown eyes; he had to be at least six-five with a body of solid muscle. Not that she'd noticed. But still, she preferred her sweet, curly-haired, handsome Quinn.

"Ursula and Valentino married Saturday and are on their honeymoon right now. He's moving from Italy to live here when he isn't traveling with his job." Nancy's mischievous eyes sparkled. "From what I hear, Crawdad Beach is a great place to find love."

Paige gave her matchmaking friend a big eye roll. "I better run before Sir Purrcevel attacks Quinn."

"Oh, one more thing," Nancy laid her hand on Paige's arm. "We had a visit from our Pharmaceutical representative today."

Paige sucked in a breath. "It wasn't Devin, was it?" The last person she wanted to see was her ex-boyfriend.

"No, but it was Clancy. He's our rep."

"Oh, no, not him." Paige's stomach churned. "He thinks he's suave, debonair, and God's gift to women and is none of those things."

Nancy's nose crinkled. "He asked about you."

Paige considered banging her head on the wall. "No. No. No. How did he find out I was in Crawdad Beach? He texted me asking me for a date, and I ignored him. I didn't want Clancy to know I'm here because that means Devin will know. Not that he would care."

"Don't worry," Nancy said. "I told him you were in a serious relationship. I wasn't lying since you and Quinn are serious friends. Besides that, there's something about Clancy that makes me uncomfortable." Nancy shuddered.

"Me too. He makes my skin crawl. I hate he's our rep. I'm grateful you're hiring Ursula. She can warn me when he's around. Maybe Valentino would be willing to make an appearance next time Clancy stops by."

"That would be entertaining." Nancy agreed with a grin. "Don't worry, I'll have Adam deal with Clancy. He doesn't need to be around you, me, or Ursula. Besides that, maybe we can hire Valentino as a bodyguard."

Paige grinned and gave Nancy a thumbs-up. "Now, that is an excellent idea."

Sir Purrcevel brushed against Quinn's legs as he set the table. He'd ordered take-out from Paige's favorite seafood restaurant. The food was warming in the oven, as her favorite ice cream chilled in the freezer. After dinner, he hoped they could sit on the couch and watch her favorite movie, which was also his favorite.

Quinn stepped back to survey the table setting. "What do you think, Purrcy? Do you think she'll like it?"

The cat meowed his approval.

"Good." Quinn checked the time. "Now, let's go set the stage for her arrival. You've got to let her rescue me, okay?"

The cat meowed and happily trotted behind Quinn as he unlocked the front door.

"When we hear Paige, I'll yell for her to help and lay on the floor. You jump on me and act like you're attacking." Quinn shook his head. What was he thinking talking to a cat like he was a human and could understand?

Sir Purrcevel stood beside him and purred.

The doorbell rang. Quinn hurried to his office and threw himself on the floor. "Help! Help!" He listened as the door opened and running footsteps echoed down the hall.

Quinn grabbed Sir Purrcevel and placed him on his chest.

The big cat purred like crazy.

"What do we have here?" Chester Taylor stood in the office doorway.

Concern in his expression, Henry peeked over his shoulder. "You okay, son?"

Quinn groaned. "Yes, I'm fine. I was hoping someone else was coming over."

Chester chuckled. "Wouldn't happen to be a gorgeous doc, now would it?"

"Maybe," Quinn muttered.

"You sure you don't need help?" Henry asked.

"No, It's okay. We were just playing." Quinn shifted but kept the cat on his chest. Sir Purrcevel was getting heavier by the second.

"Quinn?" Paige's worried voice came from the entry. "Are you home? The front door was open."

"In here!" Chester called.

Still on Quinn's chest, Sir Purrcevel rolled over on his back and meowed a pitiful meow.

Paige rushed into the room and dropped to her knees. "You poor baby."

Quinn moaned and gave her a pitiful look. "Poor me."

She popped him on the arm. "Not you silly, what's wrong with Sir Purrcevel?"

The cat meowed a moan and acted like he was the one hurt.

Quinn's mouth dropped open. So much for his plan. He gave the stink eye to Sir Purrcevel. "He's fine. We were just playing."

"You shouldn't play so rough." Paige lifted the big cat from Quinn's chest and cradled him in her arms.

"Yeah, Quinn." The poor kitty." Chester gave a sad shake of his head, but his mischievous smile crinkled the corners of his eyes.

"Paige, really. Sir Purrcevel is okay." Quinn got to his feet and shook his head. He turned to the men. "Guys, tell them the cat is fine."

Obviously enjoying the situation way too much, Chester held up his hand. "We don't get involved in domestic disputes. Come on, Henry, we best leave them alone."

"Paige," Henry said. "Quinn wasn't rough with Sir Purrcevel."

"He better not be," Paige frowned at Quinn.

Sir Purrcevel gazed into her eyes, mewed something that sounded quite pitiful, and then purred.

Paige hugged him to her chest. "Come on, baby. I'll take care of you."

"You two have a nice night," Chester said with a laugh.

The men left and Quinn followed behind Paige to the family room. He felt like he'd been caught doing something he shouldn't. Quinn was the innocent one. How dare the cat pretend to be hurt.

Then again, he'd planned to make Paige think he was the one wounded. Quinn grimaced. Either he was a bad influence on the cat, or Sir Purrcevel had outsmarted him.

He watched Paige as she stroked the cat's fur and whispered sweet nothings in his furry ear. He couldn't believe he was jealous of a cat. "When you're finished loving on Sir Purrcevel, I have dinner in the oven."

Paige nuzzled her face into Sir Purrcevel's fur. "I'll be back to check on you." She stood and scowled at Quinn. "I thought better of you."

"Seriously?" Quinn held up his hands. "You believe the cat over me?"

"He's an animal." Her eyes narrowed. "Why would he pretend to be hurt unless he was really hurt?"

Quinn glared at them both. How could he prove the cat was a super intellectual feline? An idea came to him. Hoping the cat would mimic him, he limped to the other side of the room, then limped back and forth.

Sir Purrcevel sat up and tilted his furry head as he watched. Jumping off the couch, he raised a front paw as though he was hurt and followed Quinn.

Quinn gave a sassy look at Paige. "I rest my case."

Paige laughed. "Oh, my goodness. I have never seen anything like that." She ran to the cat and scooped him into her arms. "You are the smartest kitty ever."

Quinn's shoulders dropped. He couldn't win. He hoped he would be the one getting her attention.

Leaving Paige and the devious feline, Quinn walked to the kitchen, took out Sir Purrcy's favorite meal, placed it in his dish, and clanged the spoon against the dish to signal the food was ready.

The cat trotted in like nothing had happened. But Quinn could have sworn the cat's meow sounded more like a chuckle.

Chapter 14

After a perfect meal with her almost-perfect friend, Paige sat beside Quinn on his couch. "Thank you for dinner. It was very sweet of you to order my favorite foods. And please forgive me for thinking you had hurt Sir Purrcevel. I can't believe he played us both. We better be careful what we say and do around him."

"I agree." Quinn shot a glance at the cat. "I thought I had a smart dog when I was a kid because he knew how to sit and play dead. But this? Sir Purrcy is at a whole other level. Did you know he plays chase and fetch with Henry's dog, Filbert?"

Paige giggled as she stroked Sir Purrcevel's fur. "That's crazy. I've got to see that."

"Henry said my aunt found Sir Purrcevel in the woods when he was a kitten. Maybe he was raised by a pack of dogs or a roaming animal trainer."

"However he was raised, he is one smart kitty."

Sir Purrcevel glanced at them both and purred.

"This is our advanced friendship two-month anniversary." Quinn put his arm around Paige's shoulder.

She nestled against him. "Ah, so that's the reason for the special meal."

"Yep. I'm thinking maybe we should take a step in our

relationship. " Quinn's eyebrows shimmied. "From advanced friendship to officially dating."

Fear and yearning tightened Paige's chest. "Exactly what would that mean?"

"I'm enjoying what we have now, but I'd like to know we're heading in the same direction."

She swallowed to moisten her dry throat. "What direction would that be?"

"Long-term, committed, and permanent."

Paige's heart quivered as happy chills shimmied across her arms. Was she ready to move forward to something more than just friendship? "Wait, you're not proposing, are you?"

Quinn's eyebrows rose to his hairline. "It did sound that way, didn't it?" He gave a nervous chuckle. "I didn't mean that. I mean, maybe in the future, but right now, I was just talking about us being more than friends."

Enjoying his obvious discomfort, she couldn't resist teasing. "More than friends?"

"Uh. Yeah, but I don't mean too far over the line. I mean..." He groaned. "I don't know what to say."

"I think I understand. And yes, I'd love to officially date you and see where our relationship leads."

"You would?" Quinn's smile beamed.

"Yes." Her gaze rested on his very kissable lips. "I've never enjoyed anyone as much as you."

"Same here. You're great." His gaze drifted to the floor before returning to her. "But, I do come with baggage."

Not wanting to discuss anything negative, Paige nudged him with her shoulder. "I have a nice set of luggage, too."

Quinn puffed out a laugh. "That was a good one. Before we take things to the next step, I probably should tell you why I moved here."

She picked at a non-existent thread on her jeans. "Do we have to share our sordid past? I'm not proud of what I've done." The last thing she wanted to do was talk about her mistakes.

Quinn raised an eyebrow. "You're not married or something like that, are you?"

"No. I've never been married."

"Good. Me neither. So, that's good. I'm not a loser or anything. I've dated women and been engaged twice, but they weren't good choices."

Paige couldn't resist teasing him. "Says the man who wants to get serious with me. What if I'm not a good choice?"

"You're not anything like them."

"How can you be sure? Who knows what I'm like behind closed doors."

Blinking, Quinn stared at her.

No longer able to hide her humor, she burst out a laugh.

He shook his head. "You are something, woman. For that, you will pay." He got to his feet and pulled her into his arms. "For your teasing, I will tease you with many kisses."

Paige sucked in a breath as Quinn kissed her forehead,

the top of her ear, her cheeks, and then settled on her lips.

Paige sighed a moan and pulled him tight against her, wanting to show him how much she loved being with him. Quinn's kisses were out of this world. *Oh. My. Goodness.* She'd never had so much fun.

Still in one another's arms, they collapsed on the couch and continued the kissing fest.

Sir Purrcevel huffed and moved to one of the chairs.

Quinn's kisses moved down her neck, teasing, kissing. With a groan, he pushed out of their embrace, jumped to his feet, and ran out of the room.

Did she do something wrong? Paige waited for a few minutes.

Sir Purrcevel looked at her like he had no clue.

When Quinn didn't return, she found him in the kitchen, standing with his head in the freezer.

"What are you doing?" Paige grinned as she stepped beside him.

He moaned and gave her an apologetic glance. "Officially dating you is going to be much harder than I thought. You're too gorgeous, too wonderful, and kiss way too good."

"I can wear my Coke bottle glasses next time we are together," Paige offered.

"Not enough." He stuck his head further into the freezer. "Your beauty isn't just on the outside. It's beyond skin deep."

Chill bumps formed on her arms, not from the freezer's cold air but from Quin's sweet words. How could he see her like that?

Quinn moved his head out and gave her the kindest smile she'd ever seen. "I love you, Paige Clark. Thank you for officially dating me."

Chapter 15

Wide-eyed, Paige stared at Quinn. He thought she was beautiful, *and* he loved her? "You're just saying that because your brain is frozen."

"No, my brain is working just fine." Quinn took her in his arms and held her close. "I love you. No doubt about it." He kissed her neck.

His cold lips touched her skin, and she squealed and wriggled out of his embrace.

His eyes twinkling, Quinn laughed an evil laugh and pursed his lips. "Want more, my pretty?"

Paige took off running, with Quinn laughing as he chased her around the house.

Sir Purrcevel ran in front of Quinn, momentarily stopping his progress. Seeing her chance, Paige ran into the guest bedroom and hid in the closet.

"Oh, Paige. Where are you?" Quinn's voice teased as his footsteps echoed down the hall. "Sir Purrcevel, do you know where Paige went?" Quinn's footsteps came closer. "Is she in here?" The cat meowed.

Traitor. Trying not to giggle, Paige backed as far as she could against the clothing.

The door opened, and Quinn grinned. "You can run, but

you can't hide." He stepped closer, his gaze roaming her face and settling on her lips. "I'm sure my lips are warm by now."

She whimpered a laugh. "You think so?"

"Only one way to find out." He lowered his mouth to hers, his kiss gentle. His hands cradled the back of her head. *Whew*! The man definitely knew how to kiss.

But she didn't need to let things go any further, and at this moment, she did *not* trust herself. Paige pushed against him. "I better go."

He ran his hand softly against her cheek. "Where do you need to go?"

"The freezer." She pushed him away and jumped off the couch.

Quinn's laughter followed her as she ran to the kitchen and thrust her head into the cold freezer. He peeked in next to her. "I guess we better be careful before we both get frostbite. It might be hard to explain to your patients."

Paige sighed as she stepped back. "Quinn, this is going to be difficult."

"What will be difficult?" He tilted his head, a cute grin on his handsome face.

"Getting close but not too close to one another. I've made too many mistakes. I have to be careful for both of our sakes." She crossed her arms, protecting her wounded heart. "I don't deserve anyone as nice as you."

"What? Are you crazy? Me? Nice? You're the nice one."

Paige released a groan. "No, I'm not. I dated a guy for six years. I wasted all that time with him. I have several medical degrees but messed up big time in the relationship department. Why would you want anything to do with me?" Paige swiped a tear escaping down her cheek.

"Why?" Quinn took her in his arms and kissed her forehead. "Because you're fun to be around, beautiful, intelligent, and a fantastic kisser. We even like the same music and movies. I can talk to you for hours and feel comfortable. Besides that, Sir Purrcevel likes you. We all belong together."

She bit her lip to stop it from trembling. "Belong together?"

"Yes. I won't rush or push you. I want to enjoy being together. Get to know one another better." He took a deep breath and blew it out as he stepped back. "Paige, I'm no catch. I left my last job because I was accused of embezzling company money."

Paige shook her head. There was no way her kind friend would ever do anything illegal. "Oh, Quinn. I don't believe it."

"Thanks for the vote of confidence. Don't worry. I did *not* take any money or do anything illegal. My ex-fiancé framed me."

Her hand flew to her mouth. "That's awful."

"You have no idea," He groaned. "I was not involved in what she did and officially cleared of all charges. But still, other people in the office looked at me differently, wondering if I had done something wrong. I couldn't stay at the company that accused me at first without a proper investigation or live in the same town anymore."

Paige's heart hurt for him. "Did she get arrested?"

Quinn scoffed. "No. Her father is a prominent politician and businessman who made the charges disappear." He grimaced and rubbed his forehead.

"I'm so sorry." Paige wrapped her arms around him. She couldn't imagine having that kind of betrayal.

He hugged her closer. "I'm sorry for the jerk of a boyfriend who used you. Tell me where he lives, and I'll send Sir Purrcevel after him."

Paige giggled at the visual. "Now, that would be funny since he's allergic to cats."

"That's even better." He cupped her face in his hands. "Paige, there's no one on earth who doesn't have mistakes in their past, except for Jesus Christ. The rest of us need forgiveness and grace. Your past is over, and I'd love to be in your future."

She whimpered. "How can you be so kind?"

"You make it easy. Or maybe it's all the catnip I've been sniffing."

She laughed and nudged his arm. "You didn't?"

"No, not really. But there may be some residual in the air from that first day I was here." Quinn's gaze softened. "Seriously though, I do love you, Paige."

Her face warmed. Could she say the words? She thought maybe, perhaps, she loved him. How could she be sure? "I..."

Quinn put his finger on her lips. "You don't have to say anything. Not until you're ready."

Paige nestled into Quinn's strong arms. She wanted to say she loved him and freely give him her heart.

But she'd been so wrong about Devin. How could she be sure about Quinn?

As much as Quinn wanted to hear Paige say she loved him, he would wait. Hopefully, soon, she would love him, too. He would never want to force her to say something she didn't mean.

To alleviate her obvious discomfort, Quinn took her hand in his. "It's probably late. I'll walk you home."

She blinked up at him, her smile wobbly. "Yeah, I've got to get up early before work."

As they strolled along the quiet streets of Crawdad Beach, Quinn kept the conversation light, telling her about his family: his Hawaiian mom and his dad, a blonde-haired white navy officer, and his five siblings. Quinn was the oldest. His four brothers, one sister, and parents still lived in Hawaii.

"I can't imagine having that many brothers and sisters," Paige said with a squeeze of his hand. "After my dad died, it was just me and my mom. Since my cousins lived in Montana, we weren't close to any other relatives."

"You're originally from Montana?"

"No, I grew up in Charlotte. My parents met in college in North Carolina. They moved to Charlotte after they married." Paige glanced his way. "With all your siblings. I bet you never were lonely."

"Having alone time was the difficult part. That's why I

took up track so that I could outrun them." He gave her a grin.

"Are you serious?" Paige stared at him wide-eyed.

"Kinda."

"If you're from Hawaii, how did you wind up in South Carolina?"

"After college, a great job opportunity came in Atlanta, so I moved."

Paige was quiet for a moment. "I'm sorry what happened with your ex-fiancé."

"Yeah, me too. But, God's showing me that even though what she did was wrong, God is working it out for good."

Paige looked over at him. "Thanks, Quinn. I need to remember that fact."

Chapter 16

Back at her apartment, Paige got ready for bed. As much as she loved hearing Quinn say he loved her, she kept thinking about what he said about God working all things for good.

She hurried to get her Bible, sat on her bed, and flipped to the verse her mom had made her memorize as a child. Romans 8:28, *God causes all things to work together for good to those who love God, to those who are called according to His purpose.*

Could it be true? Would God work something good in her life, even with her wasted years with Devin? She always considered that verse only applied to people who had terrible things happen that didn't deserve something bad, and *then* God would work it out for good.

What about someone like her? The verse said God worked for good those who love God and are called according to His purpose. Paige sighed. God might be loving, but she hadn't been loving toward God. How did she know if He called her for His purpose?

Paige crawled into bed. She didn't deserve God's goodness. Devin used her, but she stayed with him of her own free will, doing things she knew were wrong in God's eyes. She looked up at the ceiling. How could God love her?

How could anything good come when she'd been the one who ran away from God?

How could God love her?

How and why did Quinn say he loved her?

Whimpering, she pulled the covers over her head. She didn't deserve to be loved.

Quinn jogged along the river trail. A light breeze rustled the leaves in the trees as early birds sang songs to welcome the day.

He'd forgotten how much he enjoyed running. Maybe Sir Purrcevel would be agreeable to being on a leash to go for walks. Quinn chuckled at the thought of having the big cat beside him.

But, who he really wanted beside him was Paige. As beautiful, fun, and intelligent as she was, why did she stay involved so long with that other guy? Then again, his sister's insecurity had kept her in a bad relationship during high school before she finally realized she deserved better.

Had Paige's dad leaving when she was a little girl caused her to cling to the wrong person? Although Quinn's college degree was in accounting, his best buddy had studied psychology. They'd spent many evenings analyzing their school friends. Quinn wasn't an expert or even a novice psychologist, but he knew enough to be very careful with Paige's wounded heart.

Quinn increased his pace, pumping his legs. God had been gracious to save him and give him new opportunities. He didn't want to mess up his relationship with God or with Paige. He'd continue praying, keep working out, complete his job with excellence, and as long as God allowed him to date Paige, he would treat her with tender care.

And maybe, just maybe, one day soon, she would return his love.

Paige assisted Dr. Abbott in checking the arm of a thirteen-year-old boy who'd hidden his injury for several days by wearing long shirts. He hadn't wanted his parents to know since his accident came from riding an old motorcycle that he'd been told not to ride.

Although the boy's arm was badly bruised, scraped, and swollen, the X-ray didn't show a broken bone. Dr. Abbott gently explained the importance of not ignoring an injury. If the boy had broken a bone and waited to seek help, he could have gotten an infection, his bone cells may have started to regrow without a proper setting, or a surgeon would have had to rebreak the bone to align it properly.

From the boy's horrified expression, Paige didn't doubt the next time he got hurt, he'd quickly tell someone.

After they left, Dr. Abbott turned to her. "Is something troubling you? Is Quinn treating you okay? Are you enjoying living in Crawdad Beach?"

"I'm fine. Quinn treats me wonderfully, and I love living and working here."

Dr. Abbott's kind eyes surveyed her. "Are you sure?"

Paige shrugged. "I'm just working through some stuff with God."

"God is good about helping us with our stuff. Like our young patient, don't wait too long when something is bothering you." Dr. Abbott motioned to the door. "Our new receptionist, Ursula, starts work today."

Paige followed Dr. Abbott down the hall. "I'm sure she will be a big help."

"Yes, she will." He stopped at one of the closed exam rooms and turned to Paige, keeping his voice low. "Nancy told me Clancy is our new pharmaceutical representative. When he comes into the office, I'll handle him. There's no reason you or any of the women need ever be around the man."

"His reputation precedes him." Paige hated the thought of the smarmy man coming around their new office. Even while she was involved with Devin, Clancy would make inappropriate comments and continued to pressure her to go out with him.

"Yes, and Clancy's reputation is not good. If he bothers any of you, I will request someone else service our office." Dr. Abbot's voice was firm.

"Maybe he'll behave." At least, she hoped so.

"We can hope and pray. I'll talk to you later." Dr. Abbott opened the exam room door and greeted his patient.

Paige glanced at her tablet to see who was next on the

schedule. Seeing she had free time, she hurried to her office and checked her phone to see if Quinn had left her a message.

Another text came from Clancy. Ugh. Would the man never stop bothering her? She cringed as she read his very long and very inappropriate text. Hoping to dissuade him from further interaction, she texted him, stating she was not interested and never would be, and he needed to stop texting her. And with that, she blocked his number.

Paige took a deep, cleansing breath. She didn't ever need to interact with Clancy again.

She rechecked her phone and saw Quinn had sent a cute text inviting her to dinner at his place, assuring her that Sir Purrcevel had agreed to be their chaperone. Now, that is the kind of message she liked to receive. She did love being with Quinn.

"Looks like you got some good news," Nancy said as she leaned against the doorframe.

Paige grinned as she put her phone back in her purse and shut her desk drawer. "I'm smiling because I'm seeing Quinn tonight. However, Clancy sent me another text. It was nasty. I replied that I would never be interested and then blocked his number."

"Good for you. Healthy boundaries are important. Some people are toxic, and Clancy is one of them. As for Quinn, I'm sure you'll enjoy your evening. He seems like such a nice young man. It's about time you dated someone like him." Nancy hugged her. "Come downstairs. Ursula is on her way."

"Great." Paige followed Nancy to the reception area just

as Ursula entered the office, followed by her new husband, the movie star, handsome Valentino.

Ursula greeted everyone, then cast an adoring glance toward Valentino. "I wanted to introduce my husband to all of you."

Looking embarrassed, he nodded his head in greeting. "We're glad to have you in Crawdad Beach."

His wife stood on her tiptoes and kissed him on his cheek. "Thank you for coming."

A tender smile on his handsome face, he kissed her back. "I'll see you this evening."

After Valentino left, Ursula turned back toward them. "He didn't want to come, but I wanted him to see where I worked and meet you all. Sometimes, people are a little intimidated by his size."

Paige chuckled. "I can see how that might happen." Later today, she'd explain to Ursula about Clancy and see if she would be willing to have Valentino stop by whenever the man came around.

Noting Nancy's mischievous smile on her face. Paige gave her a quick nod because her friend was probably thinking the same thing.

Chapter 17

Quinn couldn't believe Filbert was actually winning a tug-of-war with Sir Purrcevel. How could the dog be strong enough to drag the cat across the family room floor?

He glanced over at Henry. "Filbert is a lot stronger than I would have thought."

"Don't be fooled for a moment. Sir Purrcevel is allowing Filbert a moment of glory."

Sure enough, the cat gave a quick tug on the rope, sending the dog flying onto the sofa. Filbert jumped to his feet, tail wagging with full force, ran back to grab the rope, and the play started all over again.

"Thank you again for letting us come over," Henry said. "I hope we didn't disturb your work."

"It's not a problem since my job has flexible hours."

"I hope you're enjoying living here and considering staying long term."

"I am on both counts."

"Good. Your decision wouldn't happen to be based on a certain nurse practitioner, would it?"

Quinn grinned. "Paige does play a big part, plus Crawdad Beach is a comfortable place to live."

"We do have a very special town with special people.

Well, we better get going before it gets too late. My granddaughter-in-love is making spaghetti tonight for dinner."

"They live in town?"

"Yes. They added a wing onto their home for my private quarters. I'm blessed to have most of my family living in the area." Henry called Filbert to his side and then smiled at Quinn. "Crawdad Beach is a great place to raise a family."

Quinn chuckled. "I'll keep that in mind."

Filbert trotted over and wagged. Quinn stroked his furry head. "Take care of Henry, Filbert."

After they left, Sir Purrcevel purred and rubbed against Quinn's legs. "You're welcome. I'm glad you had fun with Filbert."

Quinn checked the time. Paige would arrive in about thirty minutes. "Let's get things ready." With the cat following behind, Quinn walked to the kitchen and turned on the oven. He'd purchased a pizza from the grocery store, doctored it with additional toppings, and had a salad ready in the refrigerator.

For the evening's entertainment, he'd purchased a popular video game that Paige mentioned she enjoyed when she was a little girl. Quinn wouldn't tell her he'd been practicing for days, hoping to beat her.

After he set the table, he walked to the front room and peeked outside. From the dark clouds in the sky, it looked like they would be in for stormy weather.

Quinn sent Paige a text offering to pick her up.

She quickly replied she was almost ready and would be over soon.

Paige couldn't wait to find out what Quinn had planned for their evening. She changed into jeans and a comfy casual shirt, locked her apartment door, and hurried down the stairs.

As she made her way down Main Street, a gust of moist air blew against her face. Paige glanced up at the darkening sky and accelerated her pace.

The afternoon had gone great. Ursula had a wonderful personality and fit right in with them. She was even agreeable to having her husband drop by anytime Clancy came to their office. Since Valentino traveled for his work, they hoped he'd be around when they needed him to make an appearance.

Lightning flashed, followed by a clap of thunder rumbling low and ominous. Rain poured from the sky as another round of thunder boomed. Fighting off old memories, Paige whimpered and ran down Quinn's street as fast as she could.

Before reaching his front porch, Quinn's door flew open. "I'm sorry. I should have come to pick you up." He wrapped her in a towel. Rain pounded on the roof as Quinn brought her inside.

A quick boom followed another flash of lightning. The power flickered, then extinguished.

Darkness pressed down on her shoulders, shrouding her in memories.

Paige shivered and moaned as she mentally transported back to when her dad left. She'd followed her dad out the door as a thunderstorm crashed around them. Paige had clung to his legs, begging him not to leave. Her dad, his eyes bloodshot, his body reeking of alcohol, had shoved her away and left her standing in the pouring rain.

"Paige, it's okay." Quinn's voice reached her, drawing her out of her dark memory. Gentle arms wrapped around her. "You're safe. I'm here."

Paige took in a shuddering breath, trying to reconnect with the present. Why couldn't she stop reliving that nightmare?

Quinn kissed the top of her head. "I won't leave you. You're okay. I've got you."

She held him tight, desperately clinging to his strength. Devin hated it when she cried and would curse and call her names if she showed any emotion he disapproved of. Paige groaned. Why had she stayed with him?

The electricity came back on, bathing them in light.

Paige took a deep breath. Stepping away from Quinn, she swept tears from her face. "I'm so sorry. Now, you're all wet too. I'm so sorry."

"Don't worry." Quinn's tender brown eyes gazed into hers. "I'm grateful I was here for you. Are you okay?"

"Sure." She shrugged and tried to smile. "Yeah."

He took her hands in his and gently squeezed her fingers. "Paige, I'm so sorry for whatever happened."

Before Paige started crying again, she hugged Quinn tight.

Safe in Quinn's arms, Paige told him what happened with her father and then even told him the entire sordid tale of her time with Devin. She'd known Devin wasn't faithful, but instead of leaving him, she tried harder and did everything he wanted so he wouldn't leave her.

Her cheeks heating in embarrassment at barring her soul, Paige pushed out of Quinn's arms and stared at the floor. "You probably don't want anything to do with me now."

"I always want to be with you." He lifted her chin. "I'm sorry for what you've been through. Paige, I'm honored that you shared a piece of your heart, and what you told me will be safely guarded. I love you. I'm not going anywhere."

Her watery eyes raised to his. "Even knowing what you know?"

"Even more so." Quinn nodded. "I'd be more worried if you said you had a perfect childhood and lived a perfect life. You sure won't hear that from me. When you meet my siblings, they probably will be more than happy to share my many mistakes."

He wanted her to meet his brothers and sisters? Paige tilted her head. "When I meet your siblings?"

"I hope you're brave enough to stay around long enough to meet my entire family. I told you I'm not going anywhere. You're stuck with me and Sir Purrcevel."

The cat meowed in agreement.

Chapter 18

Even with her embarrassing, emotional outburst and telling Quinn things she'd never told anyone, the evening had been wonderful, and somehow, he still loved her.

Smiling, Paige flipped off the lights and sank into her bed as she replayed the sweet memory of their evening. He'd given her a pair of his sweatpants and a t-shirt to wear while her clothes dried in the dryer. They'd eaten pizza and played a video game she hadn't seen since she was a kid. What made it even more enjoyable was that she won every round.

She giggled, remembering how he'd acted during their game time. Quinn wasn't a sore loser; he even made his losing fun.

After that, they talked for hours. Quinn told her what he learned from his time with God about dealing with his past. Then he drove her home, kissed her good night, and promised to see her tomorrow.

How did she get so lucky to meet a nice guy like Quinn? Would God help her like Quinn said he was helped?

Paige stared at the ceiling. "God? Could you help me, too?" She waited.

Nothing.

She should have known God would ignore her.

How many times had she prayed her dad would stop drinking? How many days had she asked God to bring her dad back? How many times did she hear her mother's cries late in the night?

Paige shoved her palms into her eyes, trying to stop her tears. If she'd been a better child, would her dad have stopped drinking and never left them? Would he still be alive?

Why didn't God help?

In her dark room and her dark life, she was alone.

Her dad left. Devin left. Even her mom had moved to Montana with her new husband. What would happen after Quinn's six months were up? Would he leave, too? She couldn't stand for anyone else to leave.

Paige stilled. Something was beeping. Not loud, just a small beep every few minutes. She got out of bed and wrapped her robe around her. Taking slow steps, she followed the sound to her kitchen.

It was coming from her refrigerator. She'd left the door open just enough it hadn't sealed. Once she closed it, the beeping stopped.

Too awake to sleep, she walked to her French doors and peered out. All was quiet. There were no cars, no people walking around on the sidewalks below, only the soft glow from the street lamps lining Main Street.

Had she heard something else? Tilting her head, she listened. A voice came from outside her but inside her.

The words came clearer this time. *I will never leave you or forsake you.*

Paige's skin pebbled as a calm feeling washed over her like nothing she'd ever experienced. "God? Is that you?"

She bowed her head, trying to still her thoughts, even her very breath. More words came... *I knit you in your mother's womb. I am a father to the fatherless. I heal the brokenhearted and bind their wounds. I love you with an everlasting love. I will never leave you or forsake you.*

Tears streaming down her face, Paige looked outside at the night sky. God loved her. It was true.

Thanking God, she lifted up her concerns, fears, and failures to Him. Taking a shuddering breath, she forgave her dad, Devin, and forgave herself.

As she continued praying, a gentle warmth rested on her shoulders, wrapping her in an embrace of love. A thread of hope-filled relief weaved through her soul.

Today was a new day, and she was a new Paige.

Eight o'clock in the morning, Quinn walked on Main Street's sidewalk toward Rolling in the Dough bakery. He hadn't slept much but still felt refreshed. Paige had been on his mind, and throughout the night, he'd prayed like crazy for her.

Quinn stepped into the crowded bakery and took a deep breath of the great smells of fresh pastries and coffee.

While he waited in line, he glanced around. On one wall was a mural of a cartoon crawdad wearing a teal apron, holding a rolling pin in one of his claws and an oven mitt in the other. An old bicycle and the other had a display cabinet of antique bakery tools hung on the other walls.

Stepping to the glass front display cases, Quinn tried to decide what he would take to Paige's office.

"What can I get you?" A young woman with light brown hair and dark brown eyes smiled at him.

Quinn pointed. "What is a crawdad claw?"

She chuckled. "Most places call it a bear claw, but since we're in Crawdad Beach, we call it a crawdad claw."

"Sounds reasonable." Quinn grinned as he chose three crawdad claws along with a variety of muffins. After he paid, he whistled as he walked to where Paige worked.

He stopped at the clinic door and adjusted the box of pastries.

A guy with a black rolling suitcase-looking thing shoved past him and went inside without offering to hold the door open for him.

Quinn internally growled as he stepped into the office.

The guy had slicked-back hair and, although slender, wore a too-tight pair of black dress pants, and even his white dress shirt was ridiculously tight. The man stood at the reception desk, leaning toward Ursula as though he was God's gift to women. "I'm free tonight if you want to go out."

"No. I'm married!" Ursula gave him a disgusted look and motioned to the waiting room chairs. "Clancy, you need to wait for Dr. Abbott."

Clancy huffed. "Why? Isn't Paige here?"

Ursula narrowed her eyes at the man. "Dr. Abbott preferred that you meet with him. Please have a seat, and I'll let him know you're here."

"That's ridiculous." The jerk stormed over to a chair and sat down.

"Quinn!" Ursula smiled and waved him over.

He tried not to act too smug as she quickly buzzed the internal door open for him. He hurried inside and ensured the lock clicked before he motioned with his hand for Ursula to join him in the hallway. Keeping his voice low, he leaned toward her. "Who is that guy?"

Ursula's nose wrinkled. "Unfortunately, he's our pharmaceutical rep," She whispered.

"I don't think I'd want anything he's peddling. Is Paige around?"

"Yes, she's with a patient right now, but you can wait for her in the break room upstairs. When she gets out, I'll let her know you're here."

"Thanks. I have some goodies if you want one."

"I do, but I'll wait until the coast is clear."

"Understood. I'll see you in a few." Quinn hurried up the stairs, went to the break room, and set the items on the table. Since they had a single-serve coffee machine, he made himself a cup and sat in a chair to wait.

Maybe he should have texted Paige to let her know he'd stop by this morning. Hopefully, she'd have a few minutes so he could make sure she was alright after last night's storm.

"Quinn, hello." Nancy Abbott came toward him. "So good

to see you. I'm sure you're here for Paige."

"Yes, but I brought pastries from the bakery." He opened the box top as he stood.

"Oh, my. You are a good man." She peeked inside. "Crawdad claws are my favorite. Thank you." She placed one on a napkin and stood next to him. "So, how are things going?"

Quinn grinned at her knowing smile. "I believe things are moving along nicely."

"Good. Adam and I have been praying for you two. We're very grateful you are treating Paige so well."

"She deserves the best. Thank you for the prayers. They are appreciated. I hope Paige will let me stay around for a long time. And I do mean a permanent time. How's she doing this morning?"

"Oh, my. That's wonderful news. Paige was in a fabulous mood. I've never seen her so happy. No, happy isn't the right word. She was absolutely joyful. Keep up the good work." Nancy hugged him.

Quinn grinned at the surprising affection. "I'll do my best." As she turned to go, he stopped her. "There's a guy named Clancy in the waiting room. Should I go down there and keep an eye on things?"

Nancy grimaced. "No, I'll get Adam. The last thing we need is Clancy loose in the building."

Quinn rubbed his chin. Who was that guy? And why did his gut tell him trouble was brewing?

Chapter 19

Paige kept a professional look as she walked her young patient with her mom to the reception area for checkout. Crawdad Beach had a surprising number of children visiting their office with scrapes and cuts. Evidently, the crawdad bandages were the talk of every child in town.

Down the hall, Paige saw Ursula grimace as she cut her eyes toward the waiting area, then back toward her. "You're needed upstairs, STAT."

Paige stopped. She knew what that meant. Clancy was in the building. She motioned the patients toward the reception area, then backpedaled and hurried to the stairs. Thank goodness she wouldn't have to see the man. Hopefully, Dr. Abbott would handle him when he was through with his next patient.

She tiptoed up the stairs and entered the break room. Paige grinned as she peeked in the box on the table. Someone had been to the bakery.

"The crawdad claws are the best."

She turned to find Quinn smiling at her. "What are you doing here?"

"I came to check on my favorite person in the world."

Paige scrunched her shoulders in pleasure. "Me?"

"Yes, you." Quinn took her in his arms and kissed her. "How are you doing today?"

"Oh, Quinn. I'm doing better than I think I've ever done."

"I do have that effect on women."

Paige lightly smacked his arm. "You are wonderful, but something amazing happened last night." She pulled him toward the table and had him sit.

She sat across from him and took a deep breath. "God showed up. I know He loves me."

Quinn's eyes shimmered. "I knew He did."

"You might have known that, but I didn't. Not really. But last night..." She jumped up, closed the door, and stood beside him. "I think God talked to me. I heard Him, not out loud or anything. Even though it was kind of outside me, it was inside me. Do you think He would do that?."

"Yes." He nodded as he stood. "God said to call to Him, and He will tell us great and mighty things we do not know, and Jesus said His sheep hear His voice. I believe God talks to us, but most of the time, we're too busy to notice, or we spend so much time telling God what we want and need that we don't give Him time to answer, or we don't stay quiet enough to listen."

"I get that." Paige nibbled on her lip. "What if I had been quieter sooner or listened better? Maybe I wouldn't have messed up so many years."

"We can't change our past, so please don't miss the moment now that God has given you. Paige, over the years, I kept beating myself up for things I did or didn't do, causing me to miss and enjoy years of my life." Quinn took her hands in his. "I memorized Isaiah 43:18-19 because it's so cool. It says, do not remember the former things, nor consider the things of old. Behold, I will do a new thing, now it shall spring forth; shall you not know it? I will even make a road in the wilderness and rivers in the desert."

Quinn's excitement contagious, he continued. "And then I read where Oswald Chambers said, 'Leave the broken, irreversible past in God's hands, and step out into the invincible future with Him.'"

"Oh, Quinn. Those are beautiful. Can we maybe do that together?"

"Together? You mean, forget the past and step into the invincible future with God?"

Paige bounced on her toes. "Yes, please!"

"That's an invitation I will not miss." He pulled her toward him and gave her a kiss that made her legs turn to jelly.

She sighed against him. "I love you."

He pulled back, his eyes wide. "You do?"

Paige nodded. "Yes. I love you, Quinn Young."

She loved him! Quinn kissed Paige again. He wanted to shout from the highest mountain that Paige Clark loved him.

"Excuse me."

At the female voice behind them, they both stepped away from one another.

Nancy stood in the doorway, grinning. "Looks like you two are getting along. I'm sorry to interrupt. Paige, Adam has a question regarding some medicine he's ordering. He's in his office. Clancy is there with him."

"Ugh." Paige visibly shuddered.

Quinn stepped in front of Paige. "From what I've seen of Clancy, I don't want her anywhere near him. I could go as her bodyguard."

Nancy laid her hand on his arm. "She'll be okay. Adam won't let Clancy misbehave. Come with me. I want you to meet someone." She turned to Paige. "Valentino is downstairs waiting."

"The day is getting better and better," Paige snickered as she pushed Quinn toward the door. "I'm sure you will thoroughly enjoy meeting Ursula's husband."

Still not comfortable leaving Paige, he gave her a quick kiss. "I'll see you after work?"

"Definitely."

Quinn followed Nancy down the stairs to the hallway leading to the reception area. He stopped in his tracks. The most muscular guy he'd ever seen was talking with Ursula. He looked like he'd stepped off the screen of an action movie.

Ursula motioned for Quinn to come closer. "This is my husband, Valentino Bandoni. Honey, this is Quinn Young."

Valentino gave a quick nod. "Nice to meet you."

Quinn shook his outstretched massive hand. "Likewise."

Valentino's gaze surveyed him. "I hear you are friends with Paige."

Under the big guy's scrutiny, Quinn felt a trickle of sweat roll down his back. "That's right." He tried to act casual. "We've been seeing one another for a few months."

"Are you taking good care of her?"

Why did he feel like he was being interrogated? "I think so. I hope so." Quinn crossed his arms, then uncrossed them. "I love her."

The man gave him a slow nod. "Good." He paused for a moment. "Clancy will be coming down soon. Would you like to stay and help me greet him?" Valentino rose to his full height, his muscles flexing under his polo shirt.

"Greet him?" Quinn chuckled as understanding dawned. "Oh, I think I know what you mean." He stood as tall as he could and puffed out his chest but still felt like a scrawny kid next to Valentino. Acting as tough as Quinn could, he waited to see what would happen.

Paige was the woman he loved, and he would do whatever was necessary to protect her.

Chapter 20

Paige couldn't stop laughing. Quinn had questioned Clancy about what exactly he did for a living -- was he a pill pusher, pill peddler, drug huckster, or drug dealer? Clancy had gotten madder and madder until Valentino let Clancy know in no uncertain terms that he'd better be extremely careful with what he said and how he acted when he visited the medical office. Clancy had shrunk before her eyes and slunk out of the office.

Valentino kissed his wife goodbye and nodded toward them. "Call anytime. If I'm in town, I'll be glad to help."

After he left, Paige grinned at Ursula. "That was so funny when you told Clancy that Valentino was known as the Eliminator. That was such a great touch."

Ursula didn't blink. "That's what he's called. What do you think he's doing flying all over the world? Valentino received the title after he took over Mia's business. He eliminates problems."

Paige's eyebrows rose as she leaned closer. "Who is Mia? And Valentino is the Eliminator?"

"Mia lives in town, and boy does she have a story. Anyway, Valentino doesn't use deadly force. Not usually." Ursula grinned and started typing on the computer.

Quinn took Paige by the arm and led her down the hall. "Did you know what Valentino did for a living?"

"No. That's not something we normally discuss. He's such a nice guy. Surely, he's not doing anything illegal."

"He always works within the law," Ursula yelled.

Quinn motioned with his chin toward the reception area. "Looks like Ursula has super hearing and is married to a superhero. I guess I don't need to worry about you when you're at work."

Paige puffed out a laugh. "I think I'll be fine. Ursula now works full-time with us, so we can instantly connect with Valentino." She gave Quinn a quick kiss. "I'll see you after work."

"How about I pick you up from your place at 5:45? We can get dinner and then walk on the beach."

"I'd like that. See you later."

Quinn stepped into the bright sunshine. At the sound of a small engine, he shielded his eyes as he looked down Main Street.

A riding lawnmower was moving slowly toward him on the road. The driver was an old woman wearing a bright purple velveteen jogging suit hunched over the wheel as though the mower was a racecar. Several people on the sidewalk waved and said hello to the woman as though seeing her was nothing unusual.

Quinn chuckled. Crawdad Beach continued to be an entertaining place.

He turned and quickly scanned the sidewalks, making sure Clancy wasn't still in town. Turning, he checked the medical office parking lot. Quinn's gaze stopped on a black Audi. Sitting inside, glaring at him, was Clancy.

The engine revved, and the car shot out of the lot, almost sideswiping Quinn. He shook his head. What a creep.

Wanting to warn Paige and her co-workers, he returned to the medical office. Since patients were in the waiting room, Quinn leaned over the counter and whispered to Ursula what had happened with Clancy.

She narrowed her eyes. "I'll let Dr. Abbott know and send a message to Valentino."

"I think it's time to cut all ties with Clancy."

"I agree. I'm sure Dr. Abbott will do the right thing. Let me give you Valentino's private number if I'm not here. Make sure you identify yourself when you text him."

Quinn entered the number on his phone, thanked her, and left the office. He'd take a long walk around town to ensure the drug jerk wasn't still in the area. Once he knew everything looked okay, Quinn returned home.

Hours later, his assignments finished for the day, he showered and got ready for his date with Paige. After ensuring Sir Purrcevel had food and a healthy amount of petting, he drove to Paige's apartment.

Quinn parked in front of her building, stepped out of his car, and glanced up at Paige's balcony. The potted flowers he'd bought her last week were in full bloom. He loved sending her presents, anything to make her smile.

He hurried up her apartment stairs. Before he could knock on her door, it swung open, and Paige's worried gaze swept over him. "Are you okay?"

Why was she concerned about him? Quinn shrugged. "Sure. I think so."

"I was so worried about you." Paige vaulted in his arms and gave him a kiss he was likely never to forget.

Extremely light-headed from her amazing show of affection, he gave her a wobbly smile. "Me? Why?"

"Ursula said Clancy almost ran you down in the parking lot."

"No worries. I'm fine. I don't know if Clancy was angry about the talk he received or if he had evil, ulterior motives. Either way, I did my ninja-fast move and thwarted his attack."

Paige grinned as one of her brows raised. "Ninja, huh?"

Trying to control his smile, he nodded. "Yes, that's just one of the many things you have yet to discover. You'll have to spend more time with me to find out the rest."

"Really? Well, in that case. I'm sticking with you like glue." She wrapped her arms around him.

"Good. Because you are not getting rid of me."

"I wouldn't want it any other way." She laid her head on his chest and sighed.

His stomach growled. How embarrassing.

Paige giggled and squirmed out of the embrace. "I guess we need to get you fed."

"Sorry about the growl. It was my inner Ninja needing sustenance."

"Well, Ninja man, let me lock up, and we can head out. And by the way, you'll be pleased to know that when Dr. Abbott heard what Clancy had done, he made phone calls to make sure he would no longer be our pharmaceutical rep. Someone else will take over in a few weeks."

"That is good news. I didn't want him anywhere around any of you. That guy has issues."

"He does." Paige locked her apartment door and walked next to him down the stairs. "I've always had an icky feeling when he's around."

"Don't ever ignore those kind of feelings." Quinn led her to his car and opened the door for her. "Anytime you need me, call or text, and I'll come running."

She sat in her seat and gazed up at him, her eyes sparkling with mischief. "I'll text my Ninja-man 911 if I ever need rescue."

Feeling like a superhero, he puffed out his chest. "I'll be happy to help anytime. Ninja-man will be ready at any hour, day or night."

Chapter 21

Paige kept her menu high to hide her laughter.

Quinn groaned. "I didn't know they would be wearing pirate costumes. Chester said the restaurant had great food."

She lowered her menu. "You should have known when Chester is involved; you needed to check with others. He came in the other day with a tiny paper cut and asked for a bandage. He wouldn't leave until we put a crawdad Band-Aid on him and gave him one to spare."

Quinn chuckled. "Chester is definitely a unique individual. Did you know he was a commanding officer in the military?"

Paige nodded. "Yes, I found that out too. He was tough, but once he retired, he decided to enjoy life to the fullest."

"Let's not wait until retirement to do that."

"Enjoy life? I'm game if you are."

"Ahoy, maties." A young guy dressed in a full pirate costume stood beside their table. "Can I bring ye a cold one to quench yer parched thirst?"

Paige snorted a laugh. "I'm sorry. I didn't mean to laugh."

The guy narrowed his eyes, but a grin played on his lips. "Shiver me timbers, a sassy lass. We have ways to deal with wenches like you." The pirate waiter turned his gaze to Quinn. "Matey, if you be needin' help with yer wench, just call. We can make her walk the plank."

Quinn rubbed his chin as though he had a beard. "I be considering yer offer. But, fer now, we be having two pints of yer best brew of sweet tea."

"Aye, aye, captain."

After the waiter left, Paige grinned at Quinn. "I think you're having way too much fun."

"I enjoy pirate movies with swashbuckling heroes sailing the high seas."

Paige wrinkled her nose. "I love the movies, but high seas, low seas, and any seas are not for me. I get seasick. I'm a landlubber and a land lover."

"You haven't had any trouble when we've gone to the ocean and hung out at the beach."

"That's different," Paige said. "Just don't put me in a boat."

He let out a long sigh. "Well, that means the amazing cruise I had planned for our marriage is out."

Paige shot straight up in her chair. "Marriage?"

Quinn's face blanched. His mouth dropped open, then closed. He groaned as he stared at her. "I don't think I meant to say that."

Her curiosity in full force, Paige leaned toward him. "Were you thinking about us getting married?"

The waiter dropped off their tea, took their orders, and left.

Quinn took a deep breath and let it out slow and easy while he tried to figure out how to answer Paige. Why had he said anything about a cruise and about getting married?

He didn't want to admit he had thought about it, and he'd even looked into what it would cost to fly to Hawaii and cruise around the islands.

Paige's curious eyes still watched him as she took a drink of her tea, then sat back in her chair, a cute, smug grin on her beautiful face.

Blast it all. Quinn internally groaned. Paige was a beautiful, wonderful woman. Of course, he wanted to marry her. But wasn't it too soon?

He was planning to date her for a few more months, and then he'd buy an expensive ring and pop the question. But now, what was he supposed to do?

Since he couldn't erase what he said, he might as well dive right in. "Yes, I was thinking about us getting married, then flying to Hawaii and cruising around the islands."

Paige's eyes went wide, and she seemed to freeze in place.

The waiter stopped by. "Yer grub be ready soon. You be needin' anythin' else?"

Quinn glanced up at him. "Got a diamond ring I could buy?"

"Sorry, matey our treasure only be fer pirates." He

chuckled as he walked away.

Quinn rubbed the back of his neck. He had screwed everything up. Paige still wasn't moving. Had she even blinked? Maybe she'd gone comatose? Could that happen?

He held out his hand toward her. "Paige?"

She jolted as though waking from a dream. "Sorry, I thought you said something about us getting married, but that couldn't be right. Right?"

Should he lie? Pretend she misheard him? No, that wouldn't work. At a tap on his shoulder, Quinn turned to see the pirate waiter standing behind him.

The guy leaned down and whispered in his ear. "I've got something for you." He handed him a toy diamond ring. "Thought you might need this to save face."

Quinn nodded his thanks. Oh man, if he went through with this idea, his mother and sister would kill him, and his brothers would never let him live down doing something so ridiculous. But Paige had agreed that they needed to enjoy the moments they were given.

He took a deep breath and smiled at her. "I want to apologize in advance for putting you in an awkward position. You heard correctly, I have been thinking about us getting married. I love you, and you love me. I shouldn't have said anything until I was ready to propose. However, I've been given an item that might suffice until proper arrangements can be made."

Paige was staring at him like he was crazy. "Marry me? Proper arrangements?"

Quinn stood and moved beside her chair, "I believe it's common for people in love to marry. Yes, I want to marry you." He went down on one knee. "Paige Clark, will you do me the honor of marrying me?" He held out the toy ring toward her.

Paige stared at him, then broke out in laughter, not just a tiny twitter of a laugh, but side-splitting laughter.

Embarrassment ignited heat in every inch of his body. Quinn groaned. This was not going the way he thought it would go. He should have waited a few months and bought an expensive, flashy diamond ring instead of offering a toy to the woman he loved.

He closed his eyes and prayed the floor would swallow him whole.

Chapter 22

Paige opened her apartment door and turned to Quinn. "I had a wonderful time tonight."

He hung his head and moaned. "I'm sorry about earlier."

"No need to apologize." Her face hurt from smiling so much. "I haven't laughed that hard in ages. The food at dinner was great, the wait staff was hilarious, and the walk on the beach was perfect."

Quinn's gaze was full of apology. "You don't have to keep the ring, you know."

"Yes, I do. It's my first engagement ring. I'm going to put it on a chain and wear it around my neck. It's your promise that we will be married and have a life together."

He took his hands in hers. "I promise to buy you a much nicer ring. And I'm sorry about the scene at the restaurant."

Paige giggled. "It was pretty funny when the waiter staff sang a pirate drinking song as they announced our engagement."

Quinn looked like he was going to be sick. "Please don't tell anyone what happened tonight. It was embarrassing enough without our friends and family finding out."

"I don't know that I'll have to tell anyone. One of the waitresses said it had already gone viral on social media."

Quinn's face paled, and he looked like he was going to pass out. "No! Please, don't let that be true." Leaning over, he gasped for breath.

She wasn't going to let her fiancé hyperventilate on her watch. Paige dragged him inside, ran to get a paper bag, and placed it over Quinn's mouth. "Breathe, slow and easy."

His head had stopped spinning, and he could finally catch his breath. Quinn groaned. This evening was the worst, the absolute worst, most embarrassing day of his life. He couldn't believe Paige had accepted his proposal. Why? All he offered her was a toy ring.

Quinn sucked in another breath. Plus, they'd been recorded, and the video posted on social media had gone viral. He'd be a laughingstock all around the world. Thank goodness he worked a remote job. But still, he'd be seen around town. Maybe he'd cut his hair super short and grow a beard. He could order almost anything online and never leave his house again.

Paige's big brown eyes stared at him, and her lip trembled. "Aren't you happy we're engaged?"

"Yes!" Quinn tossed aside the paper bag. "I'm thrilled you said yes." He took her in his arms and held her close. "I love you, Paige. Thank you for agreeing to be my wife. I promise to buy you a big diamond ring. You can have whatever kind of wedding you want, and we'll go wherever you want on our honeymoon, and we can stay at my house, or I'll get you a new one. You deserve the best."

Paige snuggled against him. "I love you, Quinn."

"I love you too." He held her close. "I can't wait until we're together."

"I'm looking forward to that. When are you thinking about getting married?"

"I thought that was the woman's job to set the date and do all that planning stuff. If it was up to me, next week would work."

"Next week?" Paige jerked back. "That would be wonderful, but we probably should plan a wedding so our family members can be here."

"We could fly to Hawaii and get married on the beach at sunset. I'll happily pay the airfare for your family to be at the ceremony."

Paige took a deep breath. "But what about our Crawdad Beach friends?"

"Hmm, that could be a problem. Maybe we could have a ceremony here in the church, then another on the beach in Hawaii."

"Two ceremonies?"

"Yep. Marrying twice is like marriage super-glue. You'll be stuck with me forever."

Paige grinned. "Would that mean two honeymoons?"

Man, he loved this woman. "Now you're talking." Quinn kissed the top of her head, forehead, cheek, and chin and settled on her sweet lips.

Paige moaned and returned his kisses.

Quinn sighed. This had to be his *best* day ever. His cell phone in his back pocket rang, along with a rapid-fire group of texts. He parted from his beautiful fiancé. "I better make sure everything is okay." He checked his cell and grimaced.

Paige's brows furrowed. "Is something wrong?"

"Nothing too terrible, other than my family saw the video." He scrolled through the texts. "My brothers think it's hilarious, and my sister and mother want to have a long talk with me. Oh, well, what's done is done. At least I got the girl." Quinn shimmied his eyebrows and gave her another kiss. "I don't want to go, but I better go. I have some explaining to do to my family."

She giggled. "You poor baby. I'll call my mom and give her a heads-up before she sees the video."

Quinn snuck another quick kiss, then hurried out the door.

Paige grinned as she fingered her faux engagement ring. She'd never been engaged before, never had the hope that someone would want to spend their life with her.

She was going to marry Quinn Young. He was so wonderful, so kind, funny, loving, and a terrific kisser. Paige sank into the couch cushions, squealed, and kicked her feet.

What kind of wedding should she plan? She didn't want

anything elaborate, only close friends and family. Going to Hawaii and marrying on the beach sounded heavenly. Her mom and her husband would probably be more than happy to fly over and join them.

Paige nibbled on her lip. If she went to Hawaii, that would mean she'd have to meet Quinn's big family. What if they didn't like her? What if his parents didn't want her to marry their son?

At the sound of a knock at her door, Paige let out a happy squeal. Maybe Quinn came back for more kisses.

She ran and opened the door.

All her warm fuzzy feelings evaporated in an instant.

Paige sucked in a breath. "What are *you* doing here?"

Quinn parked his car in his driveway but didn't get out. Maybe he should have stayed longer with Paige and discussed their wedding plans. If she was open to flying to Hawaii for the ceremony, that might distract his family from his embarrassing proposal.

They would be thrilled he was engaged, and he had no doubt they would love Paige, but he had a feeling that viral video would haunt him forever.

He put the car in reverse and drove back to her apartment building. When he arrived, he parked next to a black Audi.

A vice gripped his chest. What if Clancy was with Paige?

Praying like crazy for her protection, Quinn took two stairs at a time and banged on her door. "Paige, it's me." He could hear noises like a scuffle.

Panicked, Quinn banged again. "Are you okay? Open up!"

The door flew open, and Clancy stood holding his nose, blood trickling through his hand. "She's all yours." He shoved past him and staggered down the stairs.

Quinn turned back to see Paige grinning, holding a bottle.

She twirled it in her hand. "After Clancy's obscene comments, I showed him what he could do with his champagne. You're not the only one with Ninja moves."

"He didn't hurt you, did he?" Quinn took her in his arms and held her tight.

"No, I didn't give him the chance. But, if you don't loosen your grip, I might suffocate." Paige chuckled as he released her.

"I'm sorry. I'm just so grateful you're okay."

"I'm fine, but thank you for coming to my rescue. How did you know he was here?"

"I wish I could say my superpowers kicked in, and I knew you were in trouble. But I just wanted to talk about wedding plans."

"Either way, I'm glad you came."

At Paige's beautiful smile, Quinn pulled her close, not too close, just enough to give her a very thorough volley of kisses.

Epilogue

A slight touch of fall colored the tree's green leaves as the evening sun cast playful shadows along the trail. The lazy river flowed, bubbling as though enjoying the day.

Paige threaded her fingers in her husband's strong hand. "I've never been happier."

"The feeling is mutual." Quinn grinned.

Sir Purrcevel, wearing his harness, happily trotted in front of them while Quinn, with his free hand, kept a firm grip on the leash.

"I love you, Paige Clark Young," Quinn squeezed her fingers.

"I love you too, Mr. Young. The ceremony was beautiful and perfect. I can't wait to see the photos and video."

"The marriage video will be much better than the engagement fiasco," He said with a groan.

"I thought it was hilarious that people recognized us even when we were in Hawaii."

Quinn shook his head but his eyes were bright with humor. "Not so funny. Even if it did make me an instant celebrity."

"It's an honor to be married to someone famous."

He puffed out his chest. "I won't go to Hollywood and be

a movie star, no matter how many want me. I'm all yours."

Barely containing her joy, she scrunched up her shoulders. "Oh, Quinn, I'm so happy. I love your family, and my mom and stepdad love you too. Plus, our engagement party here in town was wonderful. I can't believe how many of the townspeople came to wish us well. Chester said we are now official Crawdadians." Paige pressed a kiss to Quinn's cheek. "Thank you for marrying me."

"Thank you for marrying *me*. You're the best wife I've ever had." His mischievous grin spread.

She nudged him with her arm. "I'm your only wife."

"That's right. The very best forever and ever." He stopped and kissed her with so many sweet kisses her legs could barely hold her up.

He whispered in her ear. "I wish we hadn't waited so long to get married."

"I agree." Paige giggled as she tried to regain her thoughts and her footing. "Waiting an *entire* month after we were engaged was torture."

"You have no idea. My electric bill was crazy high since I spent so much time with my head stuck in the freezer."

She gave him her sauciest smile. "You don't have to worry about that anymore."

"No, I don't." Quinn gave her a cute growl.

Sir Purrcevel pulled on his leash, jolting Quinn's arm. He stumbled forward. "I guess we need to keep moving."

"I still can't believe he enjoys taking walks and was okay wearing a harness."

Quinn leaned closer, his voice quiet. "He's great unless he sees a s. q. u. i. r. r. e. l."

Paige couldn't resist. She knew what would happen if the big cat heard the word. "Did you say squirrel?"

Quinn yelped as Sir Purrcevel charged off, dragging him down the trail.

Paige giggled as she ran after them. God had blessed her in so many ways she couldn't keep count. She thought she was running from her problems when she moved to Crawdad Beach.

Instead, she'd run straight into God's forever love.

The End

A New Paige

Acknowledgments

Thank You, Heavenly Father, for blessing me with the interesting, sometimes quirky, and entertaining characters of Crawdad Beach. Thank You that You are a God who gives new opportunities and new mercies every single day.

My sweet husband, Dennis, thank you for loving and marrying me. Thank You for your help, support, and encouragement. I'm so grateful God blessed me with you. I love you!

Patricia (Pacjac) Carroll, thank you again for the critiques, feedback, and fun assistance. Thank you.

JoAnn Durgin, thank you for creating the beautiful cover. You are a blessing.

Jack Foster, thank you again for your creative Crawdad drawings used throughout the Crawdad Beach Series. (Please visit Jack at jackfosterart.com).

Readers, I am very grateful to each of you. Thank you for taking the time to read *A New Paige*.

If you liked the novel, would you be so kind as to leave a positive review and tell your friends? Thank you!

About the Author

Lisa Buffaloe is a happily married mom, speaker, and multi-published author. Lisa enjoys spending time with God, Bible study, writing, hanging out with her sweet husband, and enjoying God's beautiful nature. Please visit Lisa at https://lisabuffaloe.com, Facebook, X(Twitter), Instagram (buffaloelisa), Amazon, or GoodReads.

Books by Lisa

Fiction

Crawdad Beach Series
Visible, yet Hidden
Running to Grace
Crystal's Journey Home
A Baker's Heart
Stella's Heart Code
River Steps Free
Mia Lets Go
A New Paige

The Masterpiece Beneath
The Fortune
Grace for the Char-Baked

Hope and Grace Series
Nadia's Hope
Prodigal Nights
Writing Her Heart
The Discovery Chapter
Open Lens

Non-Fiction

Float by Faith
Heart and Soul Medication
Time with The Timeless One
The Forgotten Resting Place
Present in His Presence
We Were Meant for Paradise
One Lit Step: Devotions for your journey
The Unnamed Devotional
Flying on His Wings
Unfailing Treasures
No Wound Too Deep For The Deep Love of Christ
Living Joyfully Free Devotional (Volumes 1 & 2)

Thank you for reading,

A New Paige

Lisa Buffaloe

www.ingramcontent.com/pod-product-compliance
Lightning Source LLC
Chambersburg PA
CBHW071348170626
46811CB00003B/1036